"I'm fascinated by your dog, curious to know if his training works out.

"And, I don't want this to come out as an insult—but I feel comfortable with you."

"Why would that be an insult?"

"I should be telling you how pretty you are. That I like your dark hair better than that fake blond look you were sporting two years ago. I should tell you how brave I think you are." He shrugged. "Something more personal and profound than you make me feel comfortable."

"Do you feel comfortable around a lot of other people?"

He pondered her insightful question and gave her an honest answer. "No. Not anymore."

Mollie stopped and tilted her gaze up to his. "Then that was a compliment. And I'll take it as one. Thank you."

K-9 DEFENDER

USA TODAY BESTSELLING AUTHOR
JULIE MILLER

Harlequin

INTRIGUE

For the trainers and staff at Dog Stars.
Thank you for helping our one-eyed Doodlebugs,
Daisy & Teddy, become all-star dogs.
Your expertise and kindness
were greatly appreciated.

Harlequin® INTRIGUE™

ISBN-13: 978-1-335-45694-6

K-9 Defender

Copyright © 2024 by Julie Miller

For questions and comments about the quality of this book, please contact us at CustomerService@Harlequin.com.

TM and ® are trademarks of Harlequin Enterprises ULC.

Harlequin Enterprises ULC
22 Adelaide St. West, 41st Floor
Toronto, Ontario M5H 4E3, Canada
www.Harlequin.com

Printed in U.S.A.

Recycling programs for this product may not exist in your area.

Julie Miller is an award-winning *USA TODAY* bestselling author of breathtaking romantic suspense—with a National Readers' Choice Award and a Daphne du Maurier Award, among other prizes. She has also earned an *RT Book Reviews* Career Achievement Award. For a complete list of her books, monthly newsletter and more, go to juliemiller.org.

Books by Julie Miller

Harlequin Intrigue

Protectors at K-9 Ranch

Shadow Survivors
K-9 Defender

Kansas City Crime Lab

K-9 Patrol
Decoding the Truth
The Evidence Next Door
Sharp Evidence

The Taylor Clan: Firehouse 13

Crime Scene Cover-Up
Dead Man District

Rescued by the Marine
Do-or-Die Bridesmaid
Personal Protection
Target on Her Back
K-9 Protector
A Stranger on Her Doorstep

Visit the Author Profile page at Harlequin.com.

CAST OF CHARACTERS

Mollie Crane—After escaping her abusive marriage, she keeps a low profile working as a waitress at Pearl's Diner. She relies on her service dog, Magnus, to help her cope with her anxiety attacks. But is her dog enough to protect her when her past tracks her down? Or will she learn to rely on the damaged detective who speaks to her heart?

Joel Standage—The KCPD detective lost nearly everything on his last undercover assignment—his life, his girlfriend and his confidence to get the job done. But a shy waitress and her goofy guard dog call him to be a warrior again.

Magnus—A misfit of a service dog.

August Di Salvo—Mollie's ex-husband.

Beau Regalio—August's bodyguard.

Kyra Schmidt—Di Salvo family attorney.

Rocky Garner—He can't keep his hands to himself.

Herb Valentino—The grouchy cook.

AJ Rodriguez—Joel's supervisor.

Jessie Caldwell—She runs K-9 Ranch.

Prologue

Two Years Ago...

"You'll always be a stupid country girl!"

Mollie Di Salvo couldn't brace for the next blow when it came. She was still woozy from the hands that had squeezed around her neck until she'd nearly passed out and collapsed to the kitchen floor. She couldn't pull her legs up fast enough and curl into a ball. She swore she heard a rib snap when Augie kicked her in the stomach.

She'd always thought anger was a fiery emotion. But as she squinted through her swollen eyelid at the eyes of her husband, she knew that anger was ice-cold.

This was the worst beating yet.

All because she'd served her granny's biscuits at the dinner party with Augie's parents, the Brewers and Mr. Hess and his date. Delicious, yes. But poor folks and country bumpkins ate biscuits. Augie was embarrassed to see them on his table. Embarrassed that the investment bankers he worked with might think he was a poor country bumpkin, too, with no sense about handling their clients' money.

Embarrassed by her.

Was she trying to sabotage this business deal? A faux

pas at this level on Kansas City's social registry could cost him and his company millions of dollars.

Or something like that. To be honest, once she'd drifted away from consciousness, she hadn't heard much of his tirade.

Now all she knew was pain.

Mollie's lungs burned and her throat throbbed as she fought to catch a deep breath. She watched as Augie knelt beside her and clasped her chin in a cruel grip, surely leaving bruises, forcing her to face him. "I'm going out." His spittle sprayed her cheek. "The staff has gone home for the night, so clean up this mess. And don't wait up for me."

She watched the polished black Italian oxfords on his feet, making sure that they were walking away from her and heading out the side door into the garage. She heard men's unintelligible voices, a car door slam, and then Augie's latest fancy sports car revving up and driving away.

Mollie pushed herself up to a sitting position and leaned back against the oven. Breathing in through her nose and out through her mouth, she mentally assessed her injuries. There'd be bruises and swelling, yes—maybe even a cracked rib. But she could survive without a trip to the ER, without telling lies to the doctor and nurses, without explaining why it wasn't safe for her to talk to the police. She just needed to catch a deep breath.

She reached beneath the neckline of her dress to clutch the engraved silver locket she always wore. To her it was more beautiful than the obnoxiously large sapphire and diamond ring on her left hand. The wedding and engagement rings were all about Augie and showing off that he was wealthy and generous. But her locket was the real prize. It had been a gift from Granny. The one link left to her past when she'd been happy and the world was full of possibilities. She'd been so naive.

She had no more illusions of love. Her Cinderella story had ended just over a year ago, only five months into her marriage. The first slap that Thanksgiving night after an endless extravaganza at his parents' estate with his entire family and many of their important friends still rang through her memory. She was an introvert by nature, and the days of prepping and late-into-the-night dining, drinking, and partying had left her physically and emotionally exhausted. When they got home, Augie wanted to celebrate their successful evening. He informed her he was horny and ready for sex. She'd kissed him, explained how tired she was and promised that, after a little rest, she'd give him a very good morning.

He'd slapped her, the move so sudden she would have thought she'd imagined it if not for the heat rapidly replacing the shocked nerves on her cheek. No one said no to August Di Salvo, especially not his low-class hick of a wife. She should be grateful for every little thing he did for her. Augie took the sex he wanted that night, and Mollie knew her dream life had irrevocably changed into a nightmare.

Between the family attorney and his parents' influence, her report to the police the next day had mysteriously disappeared. And the one after that had been pleaded down to a public disturbance and dismissed with a fine.

So, she'd stopped calling the police. She stopped sharing a bedroom with her husband. And she stopped feeling hope.

Now, thankfully, Augie got most of his sex from the string of affairs he had. But Mollie didn't care that he was cheating on her.

She didn't have emotions anymore.

She drew in another painful breath. That wasn't exactly true.

She had fear.

Fear was her constant companion. If Augie wasn't with her, then she knew one of his friends or beefy bodyguards or even someone from the office or their home staff was watching her. The beautiful trophy wife who straightened her hair and dyed it blond because her husband didn't think her natural dark curls looked sophisticated. Who wore heels that pinched her feet because he thought they made her look sexy. Who'd married a man because she'd believed the Di Salvo family taking her in, and Augie supporting her through the worst time of her life, meant they loved her.

How could a smart woman be so foolish? Her loneliness and despair had led to some disastrous choices.

Her granny must be turning over in her grave to see how frightened and abused she had become. She'd grown up without parents, thanks to a rainy-night highway accident when she was four. But she'd been raised with love and enough food to eat, and she'd been taught a solid work ethic and some old-fashioned common sense by her grandmother, Lucy Belle Crane. She was the girl who'd overcome the poor circumstances of her Ozarks upbringing to earn scholarships and work her way through college at the University of Missouri. She had a degree in math education, a year in the classroom under her belt, and a semester's worth of classes toward her Master's degree.

Yet here she was, huddled on the kitchen floor of August Di Salvo's big, beautiful house, afraid to stand her ground with Augie, afraid to call the police, afraid to ask anyone for help, afraid to pursue a teaching job or further her education, afraid to leave, afraid to stay. Afraid. Afraid. Afraid.

Feeling an imagined warmth radiating from the locket in her hand, she pressed a kiss to the silver oval and dropped it inside the front of her dress. Then she braced one hand on the oven behind her and reached up to grasp the granite countertop on the island across from her.

The door to the garage swung open. Mollie gasped in fear and plopped down on her butt. The movement jarred her sore ribs, and she grabbed her side, biting down on a moan of pain and bracing herself for another round of degrading words and hard blows from her husband.

Only, she didn't recognize the man in the black uniform suit and tie who wandered into the kitchen, surveyed the entire area, then rushed to her side when he saw her on the cold tile floor.

He reached for her with a big, scarred hand. "Let me help you."

"No, I…" But he was already pulling her to her feet. He wound a sturdy arm around her waist and led her around the island, where he pulled out a stool and helped her to sit.

"Looks like you took a pretty good blow to the head." His gaze darted to the placement of her hand above her waist. "Did you hit your side, too? Do you want me to call 9-1-1? Or I could drive you to the hospital myself."

"No. I'll be fine. I'm just—" the well-rehearsed word tasted like bile on her tongue "—clumsy."

She smiled until she saw his gaze linger on the marks she knew would be visible on her neck. "You didn't fall."

The man was too observant for his own good. The others had been trained to look the other way. Mollie realized she was still holding on to his hand, where it rested on the countertop. She popped her grip open and turned away to pull her long golden hair off her cheek and tuck it behind her ear. "You're new here."

Although he frowned at the cool wall of diversion and denial she was erecting between them, he thankfully retreated a step to give her the distance she needed to pull herself together. "I'm Mr. Di Salvo's new driver. He took the convertible out himself, said he didn't need me tonight. But I'm on shift until midnight. It's kind of chilly just sitting out in the garage waiting to work. I was told I could come into the house to get some hot coffee."

"Of course. Everything you need is right here. Regular, decaf. Cream, sugar." Moving slowly, but with a sense of purpose, she climbed off the stool and showed him the coffee bar tucked in beside the refrigerator at the end of the row of cabinets. Ever the consummate hostess, she opened the cabinet above the coffee makers, but winced when she reached for the mug above her.

He was at her side in an instant, grasping the mug and pulling it down for her. "Ma'am, you don't have to wait on me. Can I at least make you an ice pack for that eye? I do have first aid training."

Ignoring his concern, or perhaps taking advantage of it by continuing this conversation at all, she asked for the smallest of favors. "Would you pull down another mug for me?"

"Sure."

When he set the mug in front of her, she poured herself some decaf coffee and cradled its heat between her trembling hands. She scooted off to the side, leaning lightly against the counter. "Please. Help yourself."

"Thanks." He poured himself a mug, fully loaded with a shot of cream.

While he fixed his drink and took a couple of sips, Mollie felt curious enough to make note of his looks. He wasn't as tall as or movie star handsome as Augie, but then, *tall, dark, and handsome* wasn't necessarily attractive in her opinion. Not anymore.

Her would-be rescuer had brown hair and golden-brown eyes that made her think of a tiger. Despite the breadth of his shoulders beneath his black suit jacket, and the unflattering buzz cut of hair that emphasized the sharp angles of his face, the man had kind eyes. Kindness was such a rarity in her small world that the softness of his amber eyes woke a desire in her that she hadn't felt for a long time now. The desire to step outside herself and do something for someone else—the way she might once have helped a friend in need—the way no one had helped her for more than a year now. "Let me give you some advice, Mr...?"

"Uh, Rostovich." Had he hesitated to share his name? "Joel Rostovich."

"Listen, Joel Rostovich. Get out. Get out of this house. Leave your job. Get away from this family as fast as you can."

He set down his coffee at her dismissal. "You need an ice pack or a raw steak for that eye. If you won't let me drive you to the ER or a police station, at least let me make sure you get to your room safely, and I'll bring you an ibuprofen." He started to pull out a business card. "If you change your mind, you can call—"

"And if you won't get out, then stay away from me. Don't talk to me unless you have orders to. Don't smile. And sure as hell, don't you be nice to me again." She tucked the card into the pocket of his jacket and rested her hand against his chest in a silent thanks for his humanity and compassion. Then she turned and slowly made her way out of the kitchen. "It'll be safer for you that way."

Chapter One

Present Day.
Summer...

"You stupid waitress." The young man swore and shoved his chair back to avoid the milk dripping off the side of the table.

"I'm sorry, sir." Mollie Crane righted the glass she'd bumped when she'd been clearing his plate and quickly pulled the towel from the waistband of her apron to mop up the spill before any of the liquid got on the customer. This was more about saving the chair and keeping the floor dry than making sure the grumpy customer wouldn't get anything on his Arabia Steamboat T-shirt from the tourist shop down the street. Nor would he slip on any wet surface.

She always carried a towel with her now. While she was more than willing to put in the hours, step out of her comfort zone to interact with customers, and ignore her aching feet, it turned out that waitressing wasn't her best thing. She startled easily, got distracted by anything or anyone unfamiliar to her, and tended to withdraw inside her head when she got stressed. Although she'd been raised in her Granny Lucy Belle's kitchen and loved to cook, serving food outside the kitchen seemed to be a skill she was still acquiring after ten months on the job. But, it was a job, she had an understanding boss, and she needed both. And when her shift wasn't a train wreck like this one, coming in a few hours early to help out while her friend and fellow server Corie Taylor went to an OB-GYN appointment to monitor her ninth month of pregnancy, she actually made pretty good tips.

Not that this self-entitled bozo would be leaving her much, if anything, now. "I'll bring you a fresh glass of milk," she offered, trying to remember that the customer was always right—even if he was being a jerk about it.

"No, you won't." His morning must have been longer than hers to see how easily he got riled over a simple accident. She wasn't even certain this was her fault. Hadn't he been pushing his plate aside when she walked up with the glass he'd ordered to go with his pie? "You'll bring me a new plate of food. Everything here is swimming in milk. It's ruined."

Everything? The man had already eaten his patty melt, save for the bottom bun, and all but two of his French fries. And the spill wasn't anywhere near his chocolate cream pie. Mollie bit down on the sarcastic retorts she wanted to spew at him. *Ungrateful man. Scammer. Spoiled rotten.* But talking back to anyone, especially a man with a short temper like this one, had been beaten out of her long ago. She might have left August Di Salvo and her nightmarish, dangerous marriage behind, but the rules of survival were too deeply ingrained in her to do anything but apologize again. "I'm sorry if there was a misunderstanding. I thought you were done with your lunch."

"Darrell, we were almost finished." His wife or girlfriend, who sat across from him, tried to placate him with a gentle reprimand.

But with a snap of his fingers, the woman fell silent and sank back into her chair.

Oh, God. Not this. Darrell wouldn't be hurting the woman later for contradicting him in public, would he? Because of Mollie's mistake? Her body tensed and her pulse thundered in her ears at the potential for violence. She quickly dropped her gaze to the woman's bare wrists, her neck, and face, looking for any subtle signs that she was being physically abused by her husband. Mollie eased a silent breath through her nose. She didn't see any obvious bruising or that the woman was holding a wrenched joint tenderly so as not to aggravate a hidden injury. But that didn't mean he wasn't verbally abusing her.

"You don't understand the kind of stress I'm under." *Augie spat the words at her, bending her backward as he tugged roughly on her hair, snapping a few strands and sending pain burning across her scalp. She'd been dressing for dinner with his parents when he walked into her bedroom to announce he was ready to leave. He'd taken one look at her carefully coiffed hair and dragged her into the bathroom to shove her face into the mirror. "I said I liked you blonde. Brown hair makes you look cheap."*

And the bottled bleach color he insisted on didn't?

"The stylist said I needed to give my hair a break from all the dying and straightening chemicals," she whispered, even though the truth wouldn't make a bit of difference to her husband. "My hair is breaking."

Mollie watched the reflection of his hand down at his side to make sure it stayed there. Although dinner with Edward and Bernadette Di Salvo wouldn't be a picnic,

*at least she knew Augie wouldn't leave any marks on her
that his parents could see. Not that they'd chastised their
son or supported Mollie in the past when he'd hurt her—if
anything had happened, it must have been her fault. They
were old money and all about appearances. So, she might
be safe from his fists and feet for the time being, but that
didn't stop Augie's cutting words.*

*"Your stylist doesn't have to look at your hair day in
and day out. I do." He finally released her, giving her a
chance to ease the crick in her neck. "You'll be wearing a
sack over your head next time I take you to bed."*

*An idle threat, since she knew he'd be sleeping with his
administrative assistant at the loft apartment he kept her
in in downtown Kansas City. But the words still hurt.*

*"I can't stand to look at you like this." Augie literally
wiped his hands on a towel, as if her natural curls had
contaminated him somehow. "You used to be so smart. I
don't understand why you can't get simple things like this
right." He tossed the towel at her and pivoted to stride out
of the room. "You'll stay home tonight. I'll tell Mother and
Father you're ill."*

Mollie sucked in a shallow breath and squeezed her eyes
shut to tamp down the urge to run away from her memories and real-life stressors to safety. Wherever that illusion
might be. Leaving her husband didn't mean leaving her
fears behind.

But she *was* smart. She was slowly amassing the tools
she needed to do better than simply survive. And beyond
her own gumption, the best tool she had was right here in
the diner with her.

Forcing her eyes open, Mollie looked across the diner
to spot her service dog, Magnus, lying in his bed at the far

end of the soda fountain counter. The sleek Belgian Malinois with the permanently flopped-over ear looked like the sharp, muscular dog that was his breed standard. But in the weeks she'd been training with him at Jessica Caldwell's K-9 Ranch just outside of Kansas City, she'd learned that, despite his athleticism, her boy was more couch potato than intimidating working machine.

"Magnus…?" She mouthed his name through trembling lips. She held out two fingers in a silent *Come* command. He was supposed to watch her, comfort her. Obey her.

Mollie frowned. Great. Magnus was facing the kitchen. He seemed to be happily relaxing, his teeth clamped around the tattered teddy bear he carried everywhere, instead of paying attention to her and hurrying to her side to calm her when she was on the verge of a panic attack, like she was now. She wasn't exactly sure what it was that Magnus responded to when she was about to lose it. But clearly, her pulse pounding in her ears, the cold, clammy feel to her skin and the short, shallow breathing weren't it.

Some therapy dog. Shouting for him wouldn't do any good. Being deaf in one ear, he might not even hear her over the noise of clinking dishes and chatty patrons. And if he did happen to look her way and respond to the visual signals she'd been practicing with him, the former K-9 Corps washout would probably frighten some of the customers when he loped across the diner to reach her.

Mollie dropped her hand to clutch the dripping towel to her chest. When she got her break later this afternoon, she'd be calling Jessica, who ran the K-9 Ranch where Mollie had gotten Magnus, and where they'd gone through several training lessons together. Jessica and she had worked hard to train Magnus to be an alert dog for Mollie. But

other than that first morning on the ranch, when the par-
tially deaf tan dog with a black face had trotted up onto
the porch and lain across her feet, indicating that he knew
she needed some help—even when her own brain was too
stressed out to recognize it—Magnus's responses to Mollie seemed to be hit-or-miss. Jessica said she wasn't being
assertive enough, that Magnus didn't see her as his pack
leader and wasn't cued in to serving her needs reliably.
Mollie imagined the dog saw her as the same weak fool
her ex-husband had. That she wasn't worth his time and
energy to take care of, so long as she met his basic needs.
In Magnus's case, that meant having food, his teddy, regular exercise, and a comfy bed to sleep in.

How did she end up so horribly alone again? She had no
family, an ex-husband who'd rather see her dead than pay
her one dime of alimony, no friends outside of work and
dog training, and a washed-up K-9 Corps dog who seemed
to think she was his service human instead of him cater-
ing to her.

"Hey!"

Now the fingers were snapping at her.

Mollie startled and swung her gaze back to the table in
front of her. "I'm sorry. What?"

"Are you going to go put in the order for my lunch again?"
the rude customer asked.

"No, she won't." Mollie saw the flash of movement between tables a split second before her boss, Melissa Kincaid, stepped up beside her. Although shorter than Mollie's
five feet six, and looking like a fairy princess with her
golden hair and delicate features, despite the scar on her
face, Melissa was a tough cookie when it came to running
her restaurant. "I'll happily gift you with the slice of pie,

but I'm not in the habit of comping meals that have already been eaten and clearly enjoyed. Would you like me to box your pie up to go? I'd be happy to," Melissa strongly suggested. She turned and smiled at Mollie, indicating she had the disgruntled customer well in hand. "Go on. Take a break. I'm sure Herb will have another order up for you in the window by the time you get back on the floor."

"I'm sorry." She mouthed the words to her boss.

"Don't be," the older woman reassured her, squeezing her shoulders in a sideways hug before nudging her away from the table. "Take five minutes. Find your calm place. Then get back to work. We're shorthanded and I really need you."

"Thank you." Mollie quickly retreated while Melissa dealt with the demanding customer. At least he hadn't put his hands on her, she reasoned, knowing she would have had a full-fledged meltdown if he had. The public knew Pearl's Diner as an eatery with a cute, nostalgic decor that served filling, yummy comfort food and award-winning desserts from early morning until late at night. But Mollie knew the truth behind the scenes—that Pearl's was a haven for women working to get back on their feet again after surviving a difficult or traumatic situation. Melissa Kincaid's first husband had been an abuser, and the original Pearl had practically adopted her, giving her a job and a way to start rebuilding her life some fifteen years earlier. Corie Taylor had been a struggling single mother whose ex was in prison. Since inheriting the diner from Pearl, Melissa had paid Pearl's generosity forward, hiring Corie and allowing her to bring her son to sit in a corner booth when she needed childcare. Both women were now happily married to good men—a KCPD detective and a KCFD firefighter, respectively—and had started new, healthy families of their own.

Mollie had once had a dream like that. But after her grandmother's death and her subsequent marriage to Augie, she was content to simply be alive and have a job. She might want more from life, but for now, survival was all that mattered. She was grateful to Melissa for giving her an apron after the Di Salvos had blackballed her name and kept her from getting a teaching job—or just about any job involving education. She was even more grateful that the petite, nearly fearless woman looked out for her when it came to rude customers, and that she allowed her to bring Magnus to work with her—even if he was the worst service dog in the history of K-9 companiondom.

Once at the sink behind the soda fountain counter, Mollie rinsed out the milky towel and draped it over the drying rack beneath the sink. Then, mostly out of sight from the customers, she knelt beside her furry partner. "Hey, baby," she cooed, making sure the dog was aware of her presence before she touched him. At least, he seemed pleased to see her. When he raised his sleek head and focused his dark eyes on her, Mollie smiled, chiding him even as she absorbed the affection he doled out. "How's my big Magnus? Taking it easy today, are we?" She scrubbed her palms along his muzzle and scratched around his ears when he turned his head into her touch. "You know, you failed rescue dog 101 a few minutes ago. Mama needed you."

As if he understood her words and wanted to apologize, he tilted his head, turning his good ear toward her and placing one big paw on her knee. He whimpered softly and laid his head in her lap. She continued to stroke the top of his head as she absorbed his body heat and focused on the inhales and exhales in his strong chest, willing his calm, currently devoted presence to seep into her psyche.

"That's it. Good boy. That's my Magnus. Mama about had a panic attack with the rude man. She needs some of your attention." She rewarded him for his supportive behavior now by picking up his teddy bear and playing a gentle game of tug-of-war with him behind the counter. She wondered if he was losing more of his hearing, or if it was her training that wasn't working out. "We're going to review our skills tonight. I need you to put your paw on me or your nose in my hand every time I'm on the verge of losing it. You keep Mama with you in the here and now, okay? Don't let me get lost in the scary places in my head." She talked softly to him, explaining his job to him as if she were teaching a student in her classroom, and he understood every word she said. "You're being such a good boy right now. We're going learn a new word this week—*consistency.*" Magnus tilted his head, as if he was curious to expand his vocabulary. "*Consistent* means every, single, time. Not just when you're in the mood to pay attention. The whole idea of being an alert dog is—"

"Hey, girlie." Herb Valentino, the perpetually grumpy septuagenarian who ran the kitchen during the daytime shift stuck his head through the order window and waved her back into the kitchen. "Stop talkin' to that mutt of yours. If you're just sittin' around, I can use some help back here gettin' orders out. I'm swamped."

Mollie cringed at the cook's nickname for any female under the age of fifty. But she'd been called a lot worse. And, it was probably better for her to stay busy and focused on something other than thoughts of Augie, violence, and a service dog who'd failed her again. Besides, she felt a sense of comfort when she worked in a kitchen—even if it was beside grumpy Herb instead of her darling late grandmother. She'd learned the old man's bark was much worse than his bite. She even had a feeling he kind of liked her working beside him, so long as she obeyed his orders and didn't mess with his recipes. Mollie gave Magnus one last pet and pushed to her feet. "Sure. Melissa only gave me a short break, but I can help get some plates out."

"Wash your hands, girlie. After pettin' that mutt, I don't want you touchin' any food."

She was already at the sink, soaping up her hands, by the time he'd finished his warning. She grabbed a towel to dry her hands and pulled on a pair of plastic gloves before moving up beside the tall, lanky man with bushy gray eyebrows and faded tattoos from his time in the Navy several decades earlier. "Reporting for duty. Put me to work."

He winked at her and did just that. Mollie spent the next several minutes loading condiments onto burgers and putting side dishes onto plates. They worked side by side, with Herb cooking and Mollie finishing plates and setting them in the warming window. She made eye contact with one of the other waitresses. "Order up!"

While the other woman filled her tray with the hot lunches and carried them out to the diners, Mollie swung her gaze over to her own section to see if Melissa was still doing okay covering her tables. She was relieved to see the rude tourist had left the diner. Everyone else at least had their drinks. She'd better get back out there to make sure their food orders were in the queue. But she stopped and stared when she spotted Melissa at the hostess stand near the door, chatting with a man who looked unsettlingly familiar.

Joel Rostovich.

Not quite six feet tall. Muscular as she remembered, yet thinner somehow. Short brown hair with beautiful golden-brown eyes that reminded her of a tiger. He needed a shave, but somehow the beard stubble that shaded his jaw and neck looked intentional—and gave his face an animalistic vibe. He wore a light blue polo shirt that exposed his beefy arms, some intricate tattoos on his forearms that disappeared beneath the sleeves of his shirt, and a mile of tanned skin that was broken up by several pale pink scars that made him look like he was no stranger to violence. He looked like a mixed martial arts fighter who'd come out of the cage on the losing end of things.

He'd worked for her husband.

He'd been kind to her.

But there was a hardness to him now. Even with the length and noise of the restaurant between them muting the actual words, she could hear a snap to his tone. She could see the wariness in his eyes that hadn't been there two years ago in the middle of the night in her kitchen prison when they'd met. And when he stepped around the hostess stand to follow Melissa to a table, she saw the badge hanging from a lanyard around his neck and the gun holstered to the waist of his khaki pants.

And she saw the cane.

Mollie frowned, a fist squeezing around her heart when she saw him move. He hadn't used a cane when they'd met two years ago. He hadn't had that slow, uneven gait, either.

She'd met him here at Pearl's Diner once again a few months back, during one of her first shifts at the restaurant. No limp then, either. He hadn't been at one of her tables, but there'd been another rude customer, a uniformed police officer who'd grabbed her, and she'd had a full-blown panic attack. Several customers had tried to come to her aid that night, including Joel. She realized he was a cop for the first time that night because he'd been wearing a standard blue KCPD uniform. She'd been too shocked to acknowledge him, although she had a feeling he recognized her, despite her different hair color, hairstyle, and working-class clothes. At least, he'd sensed something familiar about her.

Mollie gasped when Melissa turned down the long aisle of tables and booths near the front windows. *No, no, no. Do not seat him in my section. Do not...*

A compactly built man with short black hair streaked with silver at his temples stood and held out a hand to greet Joel. With a nod, if not a smile for the hostess, Joel shook the other man's hand before sliding into the booth across from him.

Mollie exhaled a worried sigh and wondered if she could get away with spending the rest of the day in the kitchen, instead of waiting tables and interacting with a man from her past.

Only, she couldn't get it out of her head that the man who'd just been seated at her table wasn't the same man she'd known before. It didn't have anything to do with him wearing a polo shirt instead of a KCPD uniform or chauffeur's suit and tie. *Softer* wasn't exactly the right word, but that man two years ago had been willing to help if she'd asked.

This man didn't look like he wanted to help anybody, like he wasn't even happy to meet the man who appeared to be an old friend for lunch. Like he wouldn't be happy to run into her again.

"Mollie." Herb's gruff reprimand made her jump and pull her gaze back to the faded gray eyes beneath his gray, bushy brows. "You're fallin' behind, girlie. Finish these plates and get back out there. Melissa's giving you the high sign."

Mollie acknowledged her boss's wave to get back out on the floor before dropping her gaze to the three plates in front of her, all waiting for fries and a bowl of whatever side they'd ordered. She checked the computer screen beside the window and dished up coleslaw and cottage cheese. She salted the fries and set the plates in the window. "Order up!"

"What's your mutt up to now?" Herb asked. He nudged his arm against hers and nodded through the pickup window.

Mollie watched Magnus pace behind the counter, his dark eyes focused on her. He scratched at the swinging door that separated the soda fountain area from the kitchen, then raised up on his hind legs, bracing his front paws on the edge of the metal sink and stretching his neck to get his nose closer to her. He repeated the entire process, whining as if he was calling her name.

Now he picked up on her stress?

Yes, baby. Come to Mama before I completely freak out in the middle of the lunch rush.

"His job," Mollie whispered. "He's finally doing his job."

Chapter Two

Joel Standage didn't think anything good could come from being summoned to a lunch meeting with his covert division supervisor, A. J. Rodriguez.

Not that he didn't like or admire the hell out of the short, muscular man who was a legend in undercover work at KCPD. A.J. had taken down more perps in his twenty years with the department—either working his own undercover operation, or training and providing support for the younger UC operators he now supervised—than just about any other detective on the force.

But Joel was barely a cop of any kind anymore. After blowing his last assignment—losing the woman he'd loved but apparently couldn't trust, and damn near his life—he'd been relegated to desk duty at the Fourth Precinct offices. And hell, it didn't seem that he was much good at even that. Poring through case files, running background checks, babysitting perps who were cooling their heels in interview rooms, and providing info support to the men and women on the front line was what cops who were turning gray or losing their hair near the end of their careers did. Intellectually, he understood those jobs provided vital services to every person wearing a badge. But emotionally, it made him feel like he was on his way out, too.

He'd made his way back after injuries that would have taken out a man who was any less fit than he'd been. But even with months of physical therapy, he knew he'd never be 100 percent again. The trouble was, he didn't know if he was at 90 percent, 75 percent or even a lousy 50 percent. And the sad fact was, he wasn't sure he wanted to find out.

He wasn't sure he cared much about being a cop anymore.

He was pretty damn sure no one else did, either. He had no close family who cared, and certainly no girlfriend, anymore.

Joel leaned his cane against the bench beside his new knee and toyed with the rolled-up napkin and silverware in front of him as he summoned a wry smile. "So, boss. To what do I owe the honor of having lunch with you?"

A.J.'s dark eyes sparkled with an amusement Joel didn't understand. "I wanted to get you out of the office, amigo. Have this meeting someplace where you couldn't hide behind your desk or computer and act like an invalid."

"I died on the operating table, A.J. I've got more metal in me now than that cherry Trans Am of yours. Technically, I *am* an invalid."

"Boo-hoo." The black-haired man leaned forward, resting his elbows on the table and steepling his fingers together. "Frankly, Joel—I wanted to see you get off your ass and get back to being the good cop I know you can be."

Well, that was straightforward enough.

He was on the verge of telling A.J. that any faith in him was misplaced when the waitress walked up to their table.

Not just any waitress. *Her.*

Mollie Di Salvo. "Hi."

Joel tilted his face up at her quiet greeting and watched her set two glasses on the table in front of them with a barely there smile. She'd changed her hair. It was shorter, curlier, darker—earthier and more natural than the straight blond tresses he remembered. But it made her big blue eyes pop like pools of cobalt against her pale skin. He'd recognize those blue eyes anywhere.

What was the ex-wife of one of Kansas City's wealthiest men doing waiting tables in the City Market District? When he'd seen her here last October, he'd assumed it was a stopgap job until her alimony money came in or she found herself a better job. But that was nine months ago. Why was she still here?

"Welcome to Pearl's Diner." Her gaze moved carefully between A.J. and him, taking in the badges and guns they wore. And the cane. And the scars. Joel shifted uncomfortably in his seat and pulled his arms beneath the table. Did she recognize the pale shadow of the man he'd been when they met two years ago? Did she feel pity for him? "Can I get you anything else to drink? Iced tea? Coffee with cream, right? Or something from our soda fountain? It *is* hot outside."

"Mrs. Di Salvo." Joel's greeting was gruff and terse. "You know how I drink my coffee? I haven't been to Pearl's in months. And you didn't wait on me then."

She shrugged. "Actually, I remember from that night at…" The barely there smile disappeared completely.

"The Di Salvo estate." They'd talked for all of ten minutes that night. Either she had an eidetic memory, or she had the kind of brain that simply recalled random details about the people she met.

"I didn't know you were a police officer then, Mr. Rostovich." She clasped her order pad between her hands and hugged it against her chest. Although her voice said cool and polite, her posture screamed tension. Maybe even fear. "Not that it would have made it easier for me to trust you. You worked for my husband. That alone meant I couldn't trust you."

Looked like she still had her survival skills down pat. Underplay her knowledge. Hide her emotions.

Joel curled his hands into fists on top of his thighs, surprised by the urge to take her hand and give her a reassuring squeeze. Or even hug her as tightly as she clutched that pen and order pad—if that would ease the discomfort radiating off her in waves. "You were doing what was necessary to protect yourself." He reassured her verbally since touching her was out of the question for far too many reasons. "And it's Standage. Joel Standage. Rostovich was a role I was playing."

"To investigate Augie?"

"Yes, ma'am." Not that it had done them any good. In the end, August Di Salvo had walked away from his trial a free man, thanks to conflicting witness statements and a technicality that had rendered other testimony—like his own—inadmissible in court. And the DA's office wasn't willing to prosecute Di Salvo again until they could put together an airtight case against him. "I'm sorry we couldn't keep him in jail."

Her soft, rose-tinted lips pressed together in a tight frown. "Augie's parents spent a lot of money to make his troubles go away."

So, the rumors of witness intimidation and bribery were probably true. Did she include herself as one of those *trou-*

bles? But again, why would she be waiting tables at a home-spun diner if she'd been paid off with Di Salvo money?

A.J. drummed his fingers on the Formica tabletop, joining the conversation. "Di Salvo? You're Mollie Di Salvo?"

Her blue gaze swung to A.J., then moved on past him to the soda fountain at the back of the seating area. Joel narrowed his gaze when he saw the blur of brown and black fur pacing behind the counter. Was that a dog in the restaurant? He looked like one of the Belgian Malinois dogs that worked in the K-9 division. Joel's frown of confusion deepened when Mollie raised her hand beside her shoulder as if she was taking an oath, and the dog sat.

The dog's dark, nearly black, eyes remained focused on her as she looked back at A.J. "That's not my name anymore. And I'd appreciate you not repeating it out loud. I'm Mollie Crane now."

More curious and faintly disappointed than he wanted to be, Joel asked, "You got remarried?"

He glanced at her ten unadorned fingers. Although, she might not be wearing a ring because of the work she did here.

"Divorced," she answered, clutching the order pad to her chest again. "Not that it's any of your business. As you might remember, that was a…bad situation for me. I went back to my maiden name."

Bad situation was an understatement. Bruises the size of a man's hands around her neck. A black eye that was swollen nearly shut. Struggling to catch her breath against the pain of a gut punch or kick. Her husband had been a bully and a bastard with work, his staff, and the woman he supposedly loved—and Joel hadn't been able to get enough intel to keep the man in prison after his arrest for a myriad of white-collar crimes. Yeah. He remembered her *bad situation*.

Although she had shadows of fatigue under her striking blue eyes, and she needed to put a few pounds on her skinny frame, he didn't see any obvious signs of violence on her today. "You okay now?"

He was obliquely aware of A.J. watching the whole interchange with curiosity.

Mollie tapped her pad with her pen, ignoring his question. "Drinks?"

Did that mean no, she wasn't okay and needed help? Or, was she dismissing him as in, *It's none of your business, Standage*?

Joel sank against the back of the booth, wondering why he cared one way or the other about her answer. He acknowledged the flutter of concern that quickened his pulse at the idea she could still be in danger, knowing he was a man who could help her. He was equally aware of the dark cloud of colossal failure that settled like an ice-cold storm front in his brain. He had no business rescuing anybody. Not anymore.

If only he'd picked up on those signs of rejection from Cici before that fateful night. He'd felt the distance growing between him and his fiancée. He'd been working too much, and he'd suspected she'd gone back to using again. But he'd been trying to make things right. He'd been in rescue mode, determined to save her from her addiction and remind her of the relationship that had once flourished between them.

Meanwhile, Cici had been using her knowledge about Joel's job as payment for the opioids that ruled her life. And when information alone was no longer enough for her suppliers, she'd fingered him as a cop working undercover in their organization. Cici hadn't survived the hell they'd put her through for keeping his identity a secret for so long. And Joel had literally died trying to save her one last time.

Joel was lost in the painful memories when A.J. spoke again. "You're right, ma'am. It's too hot for coffee today. I'll take iced tea. Plenty of ice. No lemon."

Those big blue eyes looked at Joel, and he nearly forgot the question. Drinks. *Get your head in the game, Standage.* "Same."

"What can I get you gentlemen to eat?" She jotted down their order, gathered their plastic menus, and left as politely and quietly as she'd come.

Joel watched her every step of the way, as she stopped and picked up some empty plates from one table, set them in a tub in a window to the kitchen, then put in their order on a computer at the far end of the soda fountain. The dog he'd noticed earlier followed her every step, then sat on his haunches beside her while she tapped the order onto the screen. Mollie's left hand slipped down to pet the dog's head. She murmured something, and the dog leaned against her. After she tapped in the last item on the screen, he watched a real smile blossom across her mouth as she dropped to her knees and hugged the dog around the shoulders. Definitely her dog, judging by the attachment the two shared.

Joel nearly smiled himself at the tender moment, when he noticed the vest the dog wore. It was more than a harness to connect a leash to. The vest had a handle, reflective tape, and the words *Service Dog* emblazoned on it.

Why did Mollie Crane need a service dog? Was she in some kind of trouble? Had she been left with a medical condition from the injuries August Di Salvo had repeatedly given her? It wouldn't be a stretch to suspect she'd been left with some kind of post-traumatic stress after surviving that marriage, either.

Joel straightened in his seat, the rusty urge to find out what was wrong and what he could do to help sparking through his veins. Only, he wasn't really much help to anybody these days. He dug his fingertips into his rebuilt legs, remembering pain without truly feeling it. He was a thirty-two-year-old man, hobbled up like he was decades older, and unable to fully trust anybody—not even himself.

What the hell kind of help did he think he could offer the prickly waitress?

He watched the tough woman push to her feet and order the dog to his bed at the end of the counter before washing her hands and carrying a tray out to another table. She'd been clear about not wanting his help two years ago. Why should he think anything had changed since then?

A.J. drew his attention back to him. "You two have a connection?"

"We met when I was working undercover for August Di Salvo. I was his driver. She was the missus. He beat the crap out of her, and I tried to help. Without success." Joel's gaze continued to track Mollie as she moved around the diner. "I couldn't get her out of that situation. To be honest, after that first night I found her with choke marks on her neck and a black eye, I didn't have much contact with her. Di Salvo kept her isolated from staff like me. I drove her a few places, but someone was always with her—Di Salvo, his parents, security. They didn't let her say much. She must have gotten herself out of the marriage somehow after I left."

"She remembers you."

"I ran into her one more time last year. Here at Pearl's.

She must have just started working. A customer—one of our boys in blue, sadly—was getting handsy with her." Joel shook his head at the memory. "Rocky Garner? He works patrol."

A.J.'s laugh held little humor. "I know him. He's not doing KCPD any favors in the PR department."

Joel knew the veteran cop's reputation, too, having researched him after the incident. He couldn't recall the exact number of times Garner had been put on report for using excessive force or being inappropriate with female suspects. But it was enough to keep him from advancing in rank. Garner had to be a decade older than Joel, and he'd yet to make sergeant or earn his detective's shield. "I tried to help, but Mollie acted like she had no clue who I was. It wasn't too long after that I went on my…last assignment." The one that had nearly got him killed, gutted him emotionally, and left him sitting at a desk at KCPD. "Didn't expect she'd still be here after all this time. I figured waiting tables was a stopgap measure for her. Until her alimony came through, or she got hired for another job." He briefly replayed that encounter in his head. "She didn't have the dog with her then, either."

Joel felt A.J. studying him and met his dark gaze with an arched eyebrow. "Think you could rekindle your acquaintance with her? Develop a friendship?"

"What?" Oh, no. His boss couldn't be asking what he thought he was. "I don't do UC work anymore, A.J. Besides, she saw me in uniform last year." He fingered the lanyard and badge hanging from his neck. "She knows I'm a cop."

"You don't have to pretend to be anything but a cop. I'm not asking you to marry the woman or infiltrate this place as a fry cook. But it couldn't hurt to chat her up and find out what she knows about Di Salvo's operation. Word on the street is that he's courting some new business associates. And not the respectable kind." A.J. leaned in again, dropping his voice to a low-pitched whisper. "We couldn't make the charges stick the last time. I'd love to have dirt on his lawyer, who got him off with a slap on the wrist, and find out how his parents got our witnesses to recant their testimony. And I'd love to find out about his dealings with Roman Hess. That guy's as dirty as they come. If we could tie those two together, we could make an arrest stick on both of them."

Joel couldn't believe what he was hearing. A.J. wasn't playing. "You want to go after the entire Di Salvo empire?"

"They play at being pillars of the community, but I think they're all dirty. At the least, they're laundering money for a half dozen criminal organizations across the country. At worst, they're making a play to control this city on the scale of Tom Pendergast in the 1920s and '30s, or the Meade family in the 2000s." The senior detective relaxed back in his seat, as if this ambitious assignment was a done deal. "I've talked this over with Chief Taylor. He's all in for launching another investigation into the Di Salvo family."

And now this meeting made sense.

"Did you know Mollie worked here when you invited me to lunch?"

A.J. didn't try to deny it. "One—you don't belong behind a desk. You've got good instincts about people—"

"That's crap."

"With the glaring exception of your ex. Otherwise, you read people. You read situations. I bet I could ask you about any person in this diner, and you could tell me their location, what they're doing, and if I need to be worried about any of them."

Maybe he could. Although, the only thing alarming him right now was this conversation. "Two—you can keep your cool when things go sideways. That's a natural talent you're wasting shuffling papers behind a desk. Three—your detective's badge is going to get rusty if you don't start actively working cases again. I don't want to lose you. KCPD doesn't want to lose you. What your woman did to you is every undercover cop's worst nightmare. But you survived. I'm sure you've got some PTSD from everything you went through—and I hope you're seeing Dr. Kilpatrick-Harrison or one of the other department counselors for that."

He was. Although he'd missed one appointment because of a conflict with his physical therapy schedule. And he had simply skipped the last two because he hated talking about the damn feelings he couldn't yet put into words.

"Did she report me for not showing up?" Joel asked, wondering if that was another reason for this meeting.

"Dr. Kilpatrick-Harrison said she was worried about you. Brought it to my attention that you keep putting off your appointments."

"Maybe I'm not interested in passing her psych eval and getting back out on the streets."

A.J. scowled. "I'm not just talking as your supervisor here, Joel. I'm talking as your friend. Don't let those bastards break you. Don't let them change the good man you are. Take this assignment. Prove to yourself that you're still a good cop. That you're still a good man who deserves to be happy. Who needs to feel useful. Who has to learn how to trust again." He paused to let his words sink in. "Like I said, this is not deep cover. You don't have to be anything but a KCPD detective. But if you could get close to Mollie Di Salvo—"

"Mollie Crane," Joel corrected.

A.J. nodded. "All I'm asking is that you get close enough to Mollie *Crane* to find out what—if anything—she knows about her ex-husband's criminal activities. If she's in the dark about him, then you're done. If you find out she can help us in any way, then we'll have another discussion about what our next step is at that time."

He'd been physically cleared to return to active duty, but he wasn't sure he was mentally ready. There was a part of him that wanted to get back into the game, but he was equally leery of misjudging the people around him so badly that he'd be setting himself up for a world of hurt. Again. Or worse, letting someone else down the way he'd failed his late girlfriend.

He visually tracked down Mollie and found her fussing impatiently with her dog, using hand signals and looking a little flustered. "I wouldn't know how to start a relationship, anymore. Real or fake."

"Find out what she cares about." A.J. turned to follow Joel's focus as Mollie fell to her knees and petted the dog, then teased him with a large gray toy that looked suspiciously like a teddy bear. "Never mind. I think your first step is pretty obvious."

"What's that?"

A.J. grinned. "Ask her about the dog."

THE MAN WITH the binoculars merged into the shadows inside his parked car. Although there was still some sun warming the sky on this late summer night, he was an expert at blending in and being overlooked, underestimated.

When he did want someone's attention, he knew how to get it. But the time wasn't right for that yet. He learned so much more, was far more successful in getting things done, when he hung back to assess a situation first—learn the players and what he might be up against. Knowledge was power. Knowing his enemy's weak points and how to exploit them gave him the control over others that he craved.

He watched the woman walking her mutt across the street, dumping the plastic bag of excrement she'd dutifully picked up in the public trash can on the sidewalk as they hurried past his position. Although her gaze was on a swivel, looking for any threats, she didn't see him.

"There you are, sweetheart." He glanced down at the crumpled photograph in his lap, then lifted his gaze to study her again. Mollie Di Salvo could change her hair color and the quality of her clothes, but she hadn't changed her face. Even without makeup, he'd know her anywhere. She exuded that natural, all-American country girl vibe that he found so prosaic. "I've got you now."

It hadn't been hard to track down her place of work. But with an unlisted, pay-by-the-minute phone number and address, it had been harder to identify where she was hiding herself these days. Her apartment was in an older, well-maintained three-story red brick building, just a few blocks from Pearl's Diner and the pocket park at City Market, where she'd exercised her dog.

His lips curled with an arrogant smile. Once, she'd been at the top of Kansas City society. Now her world had shrunk to three city blocks.

She pulled a key card from the purse slung over her shoulder before crossing the street and approaching her building. He'd get inside another time to locate her exact apartment. For now, he was learning her routine. Did she work the same schedule at the diner every day? Walk the same route home every night? Did she drive a car? Take public transportation? Was she seeing anyone? Who were her friends?

Was that mangy wannabe police dog with her 24/7?

Did she think that reject of a mutt was going to protect her? When the time came, if he couldn't distract the dog with a steak, he'd shoot the mutt. He had plans for Miss Mollie, and he didn't want to be interrupted by man or beast.

She'd dishonored the Di Salvo family. Maybe she even thought she had outsmarted them. No Di Salvo, and no one who had ever worked for them, would tolerate what she'd done for long. If she didn't know there was a target on her back, she was sadly oblivious.

He could play this game for a while. Have fun with her. Edward and Bernadette would be so pleased with his initiative. And if he wasn't amply rewarded by the people who were supposed to respect him, then he'd take what he was missing out of Miss Mollie's hide.

He might get in trouble for it. But the satisfaction would be so worth it.

Besides, he'd have to get caught first.

And no one had ever been able to take him down.

Chapter Three

Even though it was his day off, and Joel could wear jeans and a T-shirt and forgo shaving his morning scruff, he still looped his badge around his neck and strapped his gun to his belt to remind himself that he didn't have to play any undercover part. If he was going to do this, he intended to be straight up-front with Mollie Crane about who and what he was.

After locking the door to his small gray bungalow, he paused for a few moments to scan up and down the block. He acknowledged his widowed neighbor out watering the flowers blooming in a riot of pots on her front porch. He recognized the cars parked in driveways, and took note of the people driving past he didn't know. His heart revved a little and his fist closed around the handle of his cane when one young man turned in the driver's seat and made eye contact with him.

But the guy kept on driving until he turned into a drive-way farther down the block. One of the teenage girls who lived there charged out the front door and hurried to climb inside the passenger side of the car. The two teens kissed, then waved to the girl's father standing in the doorway be-fore backing out of the drive and heading on their way. Not the enemy. Not a contact from his past. Not a threat marking him for death.

Forcing his heartbeat to slow, he headed down the concrete steps and crossed to the faded red Chevy pickup in the driveway. Mentally, he knew the older neighborhood of Brookside, south of downtown Kansas City, was a decent, safe place to live. He'd hoped to move Cici in one day, get married, and start a family together. But she hadn't wanted him to save her. Emotionally, he still felt the loss of that pipe dream—she'd loved the drugs more than she loved him. He understood now not to take anything or anyone at face value. Everyone had secrets they were willing to die for—or kill for—to keep. And he wasn't going to be blindsided by putting his trust in the wrong person again.

He opened the truck door and shoved his cane across the bench seat. The plain metal stick was more of a mental crutch than a physical one these days, but when his muscles got achy from overuse or a change in the weather, he liked to have it with him to keep from limping along like an old man, or worse, falling flat on his face. He'd briefly considered playing up his wounded warrior status to gain Mollie's sympathy and develop a relationship in which she felt compelled to take care of him and thus spend more time with him.

But the small print on his man card didn't want her to see him that way—weak, damaged, something less. He wanted to be the man he used to be around her—sharp, confident, a few steps ahead of everyone else in the room. He thought Mollie was pretty. She seemed quiet and sweet, if understandably skittish about men. And though she wasn't acting much like it now, the woman he'd met that night at the Di Salvo estate had a backbone of steel. All things he would have been attracted to if he hadn't been burned so badly by Cici—things he was *still* attracted to if he was honest with himself. It was his faith in his own judgment and ability to handle a relationship that he needed to shore up before he got involved with another woman.

Not that he was getting involved with Mollie Crane.

Not an undercover op. He didn't have to watch his back or keep an eye out for whomever might trade his life for another fix. He was a cop, straight up. Just a cop following up on his supervisor's strongly worded suggestion that he strike up a friendship with one Mollie Crane, previously Di Salvo, and see if he could get any inside information on a man who'd gotten away with breaking numerous laws and hurting too many people for way too long. Joel had to remember to look at this as if he was cultivating a CI, a confidential informant, who might be able to help the department build a case against her ex.

This absolutely was not a date. Or the prelude to one.

But he had to admit he was a little bit excited—and a little bit nervous—about cultivating a relationship with Mollie. Not unlike the way he'd felt years ago in high school when he'd worked up the courage to ask the girl he liked out on his first date.

Not a date!

Reminding himself to stay in the moment and not worry about any suspicions or self-doubts, Joel climbed inside the pickup that was as up-to-date and well taken care of under the hood as it was beat-up on the outside. He loved how the engine purred with power when he turned over the ignition. His face relaxed with a genuine smile. At least one part of him hadn't been shredded by the incident with Cici. He loved working on engines in his spare time and had done a bang-up job restoring his truck and keeping it running like a dream under the hood. Giving himself a mental slap on the back, he backed out of the driveway and headed toward the City Market north of downtown. Ten minutes later, he was pulling into a parking space around the corner from Pearl's Diner.

Leaning on his cane, he took a couple of deep breaths. He'd timed his arrival for what he hoped was the end of the lunch rush so that Mollie wouldn't be too distracted by work. Plus, there'd be a smaller audience to see him and give him grief back at the Precinct offices, if his efforts to get better acquainted with the blue-eyed waitress crashed and burned. There always seemed to be someone from KCPD here, thanks to the diner's location, its early and late hours, and its delicious, homestyle food.

Taking one last deep breath, Joel pulled open the door to the diner and walked up to the petite blonde who was wiping down menus at the hostess stand. "Mrs. Kincaid?"

She looked up and studied him from head to toe, taking in his casual dress, his gun and his badge number before she met his gaze again. "Detective Standage, is it?"

"Yes, ma'am. I wasn't sure you remembered me."

"You're A.J.'s friend."

He smirked before correcting her. "He's my boss, actually. But yes, I met him here the other day."

"I remember." She tucked the menus away, save for one. "You're here by yourself today?" When he nodded, she turned away and headed toward a small table. "This way."

"Could you seat me in Mollie's section?" With a quick scan of the diner, he didn't immediately spot the curly-haired waitress. A brief moment of panic that he hadn't been smart enough to check to see if she was working today quickly passed when he saw the Belgian Malinois curled up asleep on his bed behind the soda fountain. He smiled. The dog wouldn't be here unless Mollie was. "I'd like to talk to her. But I'll order food if I need to. I don't want to get her in trouble."

The diner owner faced him again. "Does she know you're coming?"

"No, ma'am. To be honest, I had to work up the courage to come here and talk to her." He tapped his leg with his cane. "I'm a little out of practice with polite society."

The petite blonde crossed her arms in front of her and canted her hips to one side, studying him again. He got the sense she was looking for something different this time. "You're interested in Mollie? In the nine months I've known her, she's never dated anyone. FYI? You've got a tough hill to climb if that's your goal."

She didn't know the half of it. "We're old acquaintances. The last few months have been tough for me. I'm looking to rekindle a friendship with someone from before that time." None of that was a lie. Although, it sure sounded like he was interested in more than a friendship with Mollie Crane.

"Are you a good man?" Melissa asked bluntly.

Joel stood up a little straighter. "I try to be. I don't know exactly what kind of man I am anymore. Like I said, I'm out of practice."

"It doesn't matter what your social skills are, Detective. You're either a good man or you're not." She arched a golden eyebrow at him. "Don't be offended if I ask my husband about you."

"Sawyer?" He'd worked some cases with the decorated detective and believed the respect he felt for Sawyer Kincaid was mutual. "I think he'd give me a decent recommendation. But I'm glad you're looking out for the people who work for you. Makes me believe Mollie's safer now than she was before."

"Good answer." Her lips curled into a full-blown smile. Strong and beautiful. No wonder his coworker was so head over heels with her. "Come on. I'll seat you at the counter. You can catch Mollie when she goes on her break in a few minutes."

"Thank you, ma'am."

She waited until he was seated on the red vinyl stool before sliding the menu in front of him. "Uh-uh. I appreciate you being polite, but I'm not old enough to be a 'ma'am.' If Sawyer vets you, and Mollie okays it, then I'm Melissa, and you're welcome here anytime."

Joel summoned a smile of his own. "Thanks."

"I'll let her know you're here."

The diner's owner pushed through the swinging door into the kitchen. She came back out a minute or so later, nodded to him, then went back to her work at the front of the restaurant.

It was another minute or so before it swung open again and Mollie stepped out. She stood there a moment before looking to her dog and summoning him to her side. The dog leaned against her thigh, and she rested her hand atop his head before taking a deep breath and finally crossing to the opposite side of the counter from him. The dog followed right beside her and sat when she stopped. "Joel?"

He stood and hooked the handle of his cane on his side of the counter. "Hey, Mollie."

Although she continued to pet the dog's head, her blue eyes tilted up to meet his. "Melissa said you wanted to speak to me?"

Joel frowned at the pulse he could see beating in her neck. "Do I make you nervous?" he asked, refusing to acknowledge that his own heart rate had increased the moment he saw her.

"Lots of things make me nervous," she confessed, twisting her lips into a wry smile. She tipped her head toward Magnus. "That's why I keep this guy with me." He was surprised when she elaborated on what exactly was making her nervous now. "I don't like surprises. I didn't know you were coming today. Is this police business?"

"Why would it be police business?" He frowned at her question. Technically, he wasn't working on an active investigation. This was more of a fact-finding mission, finding out for A.J. if there was any new, compelling information that warranted launching a new investigation. Unless *Mollie* was expecting to be contacted by someone from KCPD? "Did something happen? Do you need a cop?"

"No," she answered quickly. "If you aren't working a case, why do you need to see me?"

Joel gave himself a mental reminder that Mollie Crane was an intelligent woman who'd proved herself a survivor. She might be nervous around him—around men—but that didn't mean she wasn't smart. He had a feeling she'd see right through any story he'd try to put over on her.

Admiring her courage to explain her reaction to him, Joel gestured to the stool beside him. "Melissa said you were ready to take a break. Would you like to sit down and have a coffee with me?"

Her uneasy reaction gave way to suspicion. "You mean like a date?"

"I mean like two people getting better acquainted, maybe even becoming friends." He leaned toward her and dropped his voice into a whisper. "I have a feeling I didn't get to meet the real Mollie two years ago. I know you didn't meet the real me."

She considered his invitation for a moment before tucking a loose curl beneath the headband she wore. "I need to take Magnus out for a walk to do his business and get some exercise."

"Around this neighborhood? By yourself?" There were a lot worse places in the city. But a woman alone on the streets of K.C.? Especially during the height of the tourist season this close to the City Market when there were hundreds of strangers, including the pickpockets and muggers who often accompanied large crowds, visiting the neighborhood? Wouldn't be his first choice if he was responsible for her safety.

But…he wasn't. *Not a date!*

"It's safe enough during the day." She offered him a slight smile that blossomed into something beautiful when she pulled a fuzzy gray teddy bear from beneath the counter and the dog danced in place beside her. "Magnus. Leash." The Belgian Malinois trotted over to his bed and came back carrying his leash in his mouth. He stood still for Mollie to attach it to his harness and was rewarded with words of praise and a short game of tug-of-war with his toy. "Besides, Magnus looks pretty scary, so no one bothers me."

Scary? With a teddy bear in his mouth? Although, the toy did look pretty mangled from where Joel was standing, so anyone who accosted Mollie might take the dog's energy, sharp teeth, and the strength of his jaw into consideration before approaching them. Instead of disparaging the ferociousness of her dog, Joel picked up his cane. "May I come with you?"

"To walk the dog?"

Ask her about the dog.

Remembering A.J.'s advice, he nodded. "I like dogs. Grew up with them. Although I haven't had one of my own since leaving home. My..." *late girlfriend didn't like them.* Nope. He wasn't going there with Mollie. He suspected the fact that he hadn't been able to keep his last girlfriend safe wouldn't earn him any trust points. "I miss being around one," he said, instead, dredging up his rusty skills that enabled him to say the right thing to the right person at the right time.

Mollie must have heard enough truth in his explanation to agree to his request to accompany her. "Okay." She thumbed over her shoulder to the kitchen. "We'll go out the back way. The alley comes out right across from the dog park where I take him during the day."

Joel nodded and followed Mollie and Magnus through the swinging door. He was inhaling the tantalizing scents of baking fruit pies and some Italian sauce sort of magic when a gravelly voice barked out, "What the hell is that mutt doin' in my kitchen? And who's this guy?"

"Language, Herb!" Joel had already stepped between Mollie and the grouchy shout when a woman with a blond ponytail waddled out from behind a bank of ovens. Her cheeks were flushed from the heat of the kitchen. She was about the same age and height as Mollie, and her arms were hugged around her very pregnant belly. She smiled at Mollie. "Whew! I wish I was going on your walk with Magnus. I feel like I'm the one baking in here."

Mollie nudged Joel aside to take the other woman's hand and squeeze it. "Didn't the doctor say you were supposed to stay off your feet as much as possible?" she chided gently. "I told you I know how to bake a good pie. My granny taught me."

The blonde woman kept hold of Mollie's hand. "Believe me, it's a lot easier to sit back here on a stool and work with the food than it is to wait tables. This little one will be here any day. I swear he's already half the size of Matt. Matt Taylor—that's my husband," she explained to Joel. "He's six-five." She rubbed her belly with her other hand as she smiled at him. "Who's your friend?"

A lanky older man with bushy gray eyebrows and an old USN tattoo on his forearm stepped up between the women. "Not my fault. I can't keep her sittin' down like she's supposed to be." He was where the growly voice had come from. "I swear to God, girlie, if you have that baby in my kitchen, *I'm* the one they'll be taking to the hospital." The words were complaints, but Joel thought he detected more of a protective papa bear in the man's stance. "You're sure he's a friend?" he asked Mollie. "You ain't never brought a man back here before. Hell, I ain't never seen you with a man, period. He ain't forcin' you to go somewhere, is he?"

Definitely a protective papa with the women who worked at the diner. "No, sir," Joel assured him, holding up his badge. "I'm one of the good guys. We're taking the dog for a walk."

"I'd like to hear that from her," he insisted.

"He's a friend, Herb." Joel glanced over to see Mollie smile at the older man. She put Magnus into a sit position, then made introductions. "Detective Joel Standage, this is my friend, Corie Taylor—responsible for all the delicious pies you've eaten here, and she's due to give birth to her second child next week."

"Not in my kitchen," the grouch with the bandanna tied around the top of his head insisted.

"And this grump is our chief cook and all-around ray of sunshine. Herb Valentino."

While Joel wanted to savor the unexpected snark in Mollie's comment and bask in the soft beauty of what he suspected was a rare smile, he remembered he was here hoping to earn Mollie's trust. Making friends with her friends seemed to be a good way to start. He extended his hand to the older man and nodded toward the faded black tattoo on his forearm. "You're a Navy man. Thank you for your service."

Herb seemed a little flustered to be acknowledged for his time in the military. But like the Navy men Joel knew best, he was proud to claim his ties to the letters and anchor inked on his arm. He reached out to shake Joel's hand. "I served twenty years on boats. Ten years on an aircraft carrier. I ran a tight mess."

"My dad was in the Gulf during Desert Storm. Marine. Demolitions expert. Defused a lot of land mines."

Herb's grip on Joel's hand tightened with a begrudging mutual respect. "He make it home?"

"Yes, sir." By the time they released hands, the cook seemed to see him as less of an intruder in his kitchen. "He stuck with it for twenty years. Now he's an accountant here in K.C. Just a few years away from his civilian retirement."

"You didn't follow him into the service?"

Joel shook his head. "No mom in the picture. She left when I was eighteen. I was the oldest of three boys. I raised my younger brothers while Dad finished up his commitment. Both my brothers serve now, though. Army National Guard and a career Marine."

"You serve our city as a police officer," Mollie pointed out from beside him.

"Yeah, I do." He glanced over at her and nodded his

thanks for her support. "Dad remarried a few years back. Sweet lady. Another accountant in his office."

Corie pointed to Mollie and grinned. "Mollie is our numbers guru here. She tutored my son through his HAL math class, that's High Ability Learner, meaning I didn't understand his pre-Calculus, and she worked out a huge snafu in the books here at the diner. The cook who was here before Herb was ordering food on the sly to supply his own pop-up restaurant—on Melissa's tab."

"Fired his ass," Herb added. "Good thing I came along when I did. These two little ladies were trying to run this kitchen on their own. With no clue how to do it for paying customers. Slow as molasses."

Corie linked her arm through Herb's. "We make good food, but we're nowhere near as fast as this guy. Like he said, he runs a tight kitchen."

"Don't make me blush, girlie," the older man groused before shooing Joel and Mollie toward the back door. "You two get on with whatever you're doin' and get that mutt out of here."

"He's a service dog," Mollie reminded the gruff cook. "I'm allowed to have him with me wherever I go. He's never bothered anything in your kitchen."

"Well, I don't have to like it. And don't be late comin' back because I'll need your help gettin' prepped for the dinner shift." He patted Corie's hand where it rested on his arm. "I'm sendin' this one home."

Mollie nodded. "I'll help until Melissa needs me out front. And Corie? Listen to Herb. Go home if you need to. Put your feet up. I can pull the pies out of the oven and do the prep work when I get back."

"And have my darling husband hovering over me

24/7? The baby's room has been ready for a month. My grandmother-in-law gave me that great baby shower. At least here I'm allowed to do something." Corie shooed them on their way, too. "Go. No matter what this guy says, the baby and I are fine. Not my first rodeo."

Mollie glanced over at Joel and tweaked her lips into another wry expression, as if she was rethinking saying yes to spending a few minutes with him. He needed to move them along before he failed his first assignment out of the office since coming back from his medical leave. "Maybe I should—"

"We'd better get going before your break is over," Joel pointed out. "Magnus needs his exercise."

Mollie nodded. "Of course, he does."

"Don't forget your key so you can get back in," Corie reminded her.

Mollie patted her apron pocket. "I've got it."

Joel nodded to the cook and baker. "Nice to meet you both." He automatically brushed his fingers across the small of Mollie's back to turn her to the back door and tried not to take it personally when she scooted away from his touch.

She peeled off her sweater and tied the sleeves around her middle, unwittingly accenting her narrow waist and the flare of her hips, before tucking the teddy bear into the waistband created by the sweater. Giving a slight tug on the leash, she urged the dog into step between them. "Magnus, heel."

More distance. But considering who she'd been married to, Joel could understand how she'd be reluctant to have a man anywhere near her. He had his work cut out for him to earn her trust. But as long as she was willing to have a conversation with him, he'd take it as a win.

Chapter Four

Joel held open the heavy steel door that led into the alley behind the diner. Magnus leaped over the concrete step onto the asphalt and Mollie followed quickly behind him.

While he was instantly assaulted with the heat and humidity of the July afternoon, goose bumps pricked along his forearms. A potential ambush was his past talking, not the here and now. But it was second nature for him to check up and down the thoroughfare between two busy side streets, ensuring it was empty of traffic and pedestrians. The dumpster and recycling bin behind the restaurant gave easy places for someone to hide, as did the light poles and recessed doorways leading into the building across the alley.

He quickly shook off his suspicions and jogged to catch up with Mollie as she and Magnus headed toward the end of the alley at a fast clip. He couldn't help but check each hidey-hole as he passed it. But there was no enemy hidden here. And despite the sketchiness of a back alley, this one was remarkably clean. Other than a collection of cigarette butts on the ground at one back door, indicating a smoking area for employees, no doubt, there was no overflowing trash piled up beside the bins and dumpsters. And it looked like it would be well lit at night, judging by the lights on the centermost pole and above every door.

His nostrils flared with a steadying breath. He should be aware of his surroundings, but being paranoid about the bogeyman or some drug dealer's enforcer lying in wait to take him down would just mess with his head and keep him from being able to protect Mollie or himself if there was a real threat.

Of course, he wasn't here as her protector. The skills were there, but they were rusty. Thank goodness, this was all about striking up a friendship. *Not a date. Not a UC op where he had to be on guard around the clock. Just get reacquainted with the woman and talk. Then set up another time to talk again.*

Mollie looked over at him when he stepped up to the other side of Magnus. "You're moving pretty well without your cane," she pointed out.

He shrugged. "It's more for emergencies—in case my leg gives out."

"Does it give out a lot?"

He didn't want to read anything in her concerned tone. "Not really. Not anymore. I've had a lot of physical therapy to rebuild my muscle tone. It's more of a mental thing. For security."

She reached down and stroked Magnus's fur. "I understand that. Here's my security blanket." They stood in awkward silence for another minute, waiting for the light to change at the corner and allow them to cross safely. "I hope Herb didn't offend you," she said. The dog had dutifully stopped when she did, although he was panting with excitement at the outing. "It took me a while to figure out his bark is worse than his bite."

Glad for the change in topic, Joel smiled. "They're protective of you. Everyone who works at the diner is."

"We're protective of each other."

The light changed, and they waited for a black Lexus with tinted windows to turn at the corner and drive past before they stepped off the curb and crossed the street to the pocket park. A couple reading a walking tour map skirted around them on the sidewalk. An older gentleman walked his miniature schnauzer out of the dog park across the street and latched the gate behind him before heading down the opposite sidewalk. Although Magnus's head swiveled on alert to both the tourists and the dog, he remained at Mollie's side unless she clicked her tongue behind her teeth and ordered Magnus into step beside her.

Although the grassy area of the dog park was only about twelve feet deep between the fence lining the sidewalk and the brick building on the opposite side, it stretched from one end of the half block to the other. There were benches and a leafy maple tree at either end, plus a waste bag dispenser and covered trash can chained to the fence near the gate.

"An urban dog playground," he mused, watching as Mollie unhooked Magnus from his leash and gave him permission to run and be off duty for a few minutes.

"I suppose so." Mollie wound his leash in her fist and headed for the shade at one end of the park. "Local fundraisers added the fake hydrant, agility ramp, and plastic barrel just last month. I imagine every dog in the neighborhood loves to come here and sniff and mark their territory."

She perched on one end of the bench and watched Magnus check out every object that was geared toward dogs, as well as the tree and bench at the far end of the park. She busied her hands with the woeful teddy bear and gave Joel a sideways glance to see if he was going to sit beside her. Taking the cue from her guarded posture, he sat at the far end of the bench, beyond arm's reach, and she inhaled a deep breath. At the same time, her tummy growled. "Oops. Sorry about that."

"Am I keeping you from eating your lunch?"

"No," she answered a little too quickly for him to believe her.

His concern was genuine. "I don't want to be the reason you don't get enough food to eat today." He thumbed over his shoulder across the street. "We can head back."

"I'll eat dinner before I go home. Or I'll box up something to take with me." She paused long enough for Magnus to come trotting back to her for pets before he nudged at the teddy bear with his nose. "Silly boy. Go get it." She tossed the bear across the grass and Magnus tore out after it. "I've lost weight since the last time you saw me, haven't I."

"Yeah. But you've still got curves in all the right places." She raised her eyebrows at that comment. Maybe he should apologize, but he'd meant what he'd said. When Magnus returned and dropped the bear into her lap, Joel held his hand out for it. "May I?" Dark brown eyes followed the bear from Mollie's hand to his. "Go get it, boy!" He hurled the bear halfway across the park and watched the athletic dog chase it down and retrieve it. "Not that I should be noticing. But hey, I'm a guy. And I just want you to be healthy."

She chuckled softly, and Joel couldn't tear his gaze away from her gentle smile. With coffee-colored curls catching in the breeze and drifting across her cheeks and jawline, her skin flushed with the heat, and not a stitch of makeup that he could detect, he was struck full force by her natural beauty.

He felt himself smiling, too. "What? What did I say to make you laugh?"

"I heard my grandmother's voice in my head when you said that. *Are you healthy, Mollie Belle? Are you taking care of yourself? Eating right?* She was a fabulous cook, and she always fed me too much. When I went off to college, those questions came up in nearly every conversation we had." She tossed Magnus's teddy bear one more time, then tucked those loose curls back into the headband she wore. He could guess by the smile, and how it wistfully faded away, that her grandmother was a special, yet sad memory for her. "I'm not starving, Joel. Admittedly, when I first started working here, I didn't have a lot of money in my bank account." She shook her head. "Who am I kidding? I didn't even have a bank account back then. But Melissa took pity on me. She fed me breakfast during the job interview. Hired me before I'd finished my coffee. I'm not the best waitress, but I can put up with Herb, so I think she keeps me around for that reason alone." Joel grinned as he was meant to. "Plus, she has a soft spot for a hard-luck case like me and Magnus. Pearl—the original owner of the diner—gave Melissa a break when she needed one. I hope to pay her generosity forward one day, too."

Any urge to smile faded. Where was Mollie's money from her divorce? Joel made a mental note to research some court records to find out if there was some sort of legal issue with her alimony. Or if Di Salvo's slick lawyer had gotten him out of paying anything, just like he'd gotten August Di Salvo off on the major charges that had been brought against him. But instead of pressing for info related to her ex right this minute, he asked, "You have enough money for food now?"

Mollie nodded. "I have an account at the Cattlemen's Bank extension over by the City Market now. And a studio apartment down the street that allows dogs. It's just stress. I don't always feel like eating."

"You have to eat to keep your strength up, Moll." He left his cane leaning against the bench and stood to play a vigorous game of tug-of-war with Magnus. Once he'd won, the high-energy Belgian Malinois danced and drooled, eager for Joel to throw the toy again. "Go get it!" Joel looked down at Mollie. "It was just an observation. I sure hope I don't sound like your grandmother."

Although it was barely a noise in her throat, he loved that she laughed again. "My granny was five foot nothing. You're a giant compared to her. Heck, so was I, and I'm only five-six. She had a beautiful, melodic voice. Not like that gravelly tone you have." She nodded to the ink sticking out beneath the sleeves of his T-shirt. "And, absolutely no tats on Granny. So, no worries that I'm confusing the two of you." He liked that she'd noticed some details about him. He also noted that the moment she started talking about her grandmother, her shoulders relaxed their stiff posture and she'd pulled a silver locket from the neckline of her uniform and was rubbing it between her fingers. "It's having somebody worrying about me that made me think of her."

Her smile disappeared abruptly, and she tucked the locket back inside her dress. "You look like you've lost weight, too. I mean you've still got muscles in all the right places, but…" She blushed as she realized she'd echoed the compliment he'd given her earlier. "Does it have something to do with your injuries?"

Joel grabbed his cane and sat again. The topic was bound to come up. And since he'd probed into her health issues, it was probably only fair that he share a bit of his recent past, too. "I was in the hospital for a couple of months. Multiple surgeries on both legs." He turned his left arm in front of him, pointing out the pink puckers of skin that marred the lines of tribal symbols and motivational words that curled around his forearm. "Some of the cuts got infected."

"That sounds horrible. What happened?" Gunshot to both his knees. A couple of thugs trying to butcher him alive while he was incapacitated. Beating what was left of him and then literally dumping him in the trash. He'd lost so much blood by the time he reached the hospital that his heart had stopped. Drug dealers didn't take kindly to cops who infiltrated their operation. When he didn't answer, Mollie came up with her own explanation. "Sounds like you were in a horrible accident."

"I got hurt working a case," he responded vaguely.

She looked as though she suspected there was more to his injuries, but he wasn't going to share the gory details. He was here to get her to talk—not the other way around.

But she had an inkling that he'd suffered more than a car accident. "Did Augie's men do that to you?" she asked in a strained whisper. She reached toward one of the scars but pulled away before making contact, and Joel regretted missing the chance to find out what her skin felt like against his. "He had a man who worked for him, Beau Regalio. Augie called him his bodyguard, but he could be—"

"I know who Beau is." An enforcer of the first order. He'd confiscated one of Beau's guns that he'd turned in as evidence, but somehow Di Salvo's lawyer had gotten the forensic report tying the weapon to a witness tampering crime tossed out on a technicality. "No, he didn't hurt me. I was done working your ex-husband's case when this happened." He hated the words coming out of his mouth. "Did Beau ever hurt you?"

Her skin blanched, and she shook her head. "That was Augie's prerogative. But Beau never looked away. It was almost like he...enjoyed the violence. You're the only one in that house who ever tried to help me."

Joel swore beneath his breath. "I should have done something more."

"No." He flinched when her compassion finally overcame her fear, and her fingertips brushed across his forearm. Her touch was soft and cool against his warm skin, but she didn't linger. "You couldn't risk blowing your cover and jeopardize your investigation. I know that now."

He nodded. "Plus, money buys a lot of loyalty. We couldn't make the major charges against your ex stick because witnesses changed their testimony and evidence simply disappeared."

"If I could have stopped Augie from hurting people..." A warm breeze caught her hair and dragged a curl across her cheek. Joel clenched his fingers around his cane to keep from reaching out to tuck it back behind her ear. "Defying him was never really an option. He made so many business deals that were shady. I'm a math teacher, not a forensic accountant. But I could tell that some of the arrangements made at meetings I overheard weren't legit. The numbers simply didn't add up. And some of his investors who reneged on a project...? They'd be at a dinner party at our house one night, and the next week I'd see their name in the business pages of the newspaper, losing their company or closing shops and laying off workers. There was even one man..." Her voice faded away. "I saw his name in the obituaries. He...killed himself."

Yeah, he knew about the man's suicide—and probably some other cases of violence related to her ex she *didn't* know about. He reached over and lightly wound his fingers around her wrist. Her wide eyes locked on to his. "Nothing August Di Salvo did is on you. You were a victim as much as anybody. I'm glad you got away from him."

It was on the tip of his tongue to ask her exactly how she had gotten away from the Di Salvo family. But even in the heat of the afternoon, he could feel the skin beneath his grasp chilling. Her cheeks paled and she reached into the neckline of her uniform again and tugged on the long silver chain to reach her locket.

As gentle as it was, he popped his grip open and pulled away. "I'm sorry. I remember that night in the diner a few months back. You don't like men touching you."

"That's not it. Well, that customer was a jerk." She moved her fingers and focus to the top of Magnus's brown and black fur. "Actually, I miss having someone touch me. But… I need to be in control of what's happening. I need time to know who the person is and why they're putting their hands on me."

He remembered her warning in the diner. "No surprises."

Visibly calming herself, she tilted her gaze back to his. "Granny used to hug me all the time. I miss the warmth and the comfort of that physical contact. Back when I was a naive newlywed with Augie, I liked when he put his arm around me, or when we'd make out—" Nope. He did not want that image in his head. "And then, he changed. Or rather, he let the real Augie out." He'd seen plenty of proof of the real Augie Di Salvo. "I hate that he ruined hugs and cuddling and even holding hands for me."

With the urge to reach for her pulsing through his fingers, Joel hated that, too. Mollie Crane was a pretty woman with a wry sense of humor and a quiet intelligence that he longed to get to know better. But understanding that his touch might be more frightening than comforting, he wrapped all ten fingers around his cane and changed the subject. "That's a pretty locket. Looks antique."

"It was Granny's. She raised me. It's one of the few things I have of hers." Her nostrils flared with a deep breath as she paused. "Augie sold, threw out, or burned the rest of the things I brought with me into the marriage. Including the house where I grew up."

Clearly her grandmother had meant the world to her. "I'm so sorry."

"He didn't see cute and adorable and a tribute to early twentieth-century architecture the way I did. He saw *old*. And *small*. He said a Di Salvo would never live in a dump like that. He didn't want anyone connecting the property to him once we were married. I didn't know he had done it until after we'd been married for a while. I was feeling homesick and had driven out to see it. He took great pride in explaining how that part of my life was over, that I was a Di Salvo now, not a hick from the Ozarks."

"He can't erase your memories. Or what your grandmother meant to you."

"It was a beautiful little cottage. Granny took such good care of it. She planted a huge garden in the back. During December, she put up enough lights and decorations to rival the Plaza lights. I loved growing up there." Tears glistened in her eyes, and Magnus rested his head in her lap, nudging at her hands. She leaned over to touch her nose to the dog's, then scrubbed her hands all around Magnus's head. "I'm okay, boy. Mama's okay."

Joel wanted to comfort her, too. But while the dog's touch was welcome, his was not. He needed to keep the conversation moving before he did something stupid like hunt down Di Salvo and burn *his* house to the ground. "So, Magnus? He's your service dog?"

She nodded, sitting up straight before tossing the teddy bear and letting Magnus chase it again.

"Post-traumatic stress?"

"He alerts when I'm about to have a panic attack. So I can get somewhere safe, make sure I pull over if I'm driving, or to comfort me to keep it from happening, like he did just now. He's supposed to, anyway. He's still in training, I guess. I feel safer when he's around, too. He can be scary when he gets fired up. Although, he's hard of hearing. He misses a few things. That's why he couldn't qualify for KCPD's K-9 Corps." Magnus trotted back and dropped the slobbery bear into her lap. "I'm sorry. I'm going on about stuff you're probably not interested in."

"Mollie, I'm interested in anything you have to say. You can talk to me. Tell me things. I'm not the bad guy here."

"I didn't think you were." She glanced up at him. "Why *are* you here?"

Suddenly, this assignment he hadn't wanted was becoming way too personal. How much truth did he share without blowing the most interesting and meaningful fifteen minutes he'd had since the night he'd lost everything? Partial truths weren't exactly a lie, were they? "I was surprised to see you still working at Pearl's Diner. I wanted to know how you've been, if you're okay. Just because I haven't seen you in a while doesn't mean I haven't thought about you. I felt guilty that I didn't do more to help you."

"I'm okay," she answered quickly in a tone he didn't quite believe. "I honestly never expected to see you again. I thought I'd left Augie's world behind me. That's my goal."

"I'm not part of that world. I'm a cop. A detective with KCPD."

"I know that now."

"You seeing anyone?" Well, hell. Where had that question come from?

She shook her head, stirring the curls against her jawline. "I don't socialize much. I go to work, go home. Go to dog training or run errands, go home again." Her question proved even more surprising. "Are *you* seeing anyone?"

That made him go to the dark side. "My girlfriend… died."

"Oh, Joel. I'm so sorry. Was it the same accident where you got hurt?"

She held his gaze for the longest time as he worked through his personal hell to find some civilized words he could share about that night. Before the words about betrayal and loss and a wasted life could come, Joel was startled from his thoughts by Magnus rising on his hind legs and propping his front paws against his chest. Instead of blue eyes, he was looking straight into the darkest of brown eyes and feeling the dog's warm pants of breath against his face.

"I'm so sorry. Magnus! Sit!" Mollie tugged on his leash, but the dog plopped down on Joel's feet and rested his head atop his thigh. "You're *my* comfort dog, you big goof."

Pulling a rusty laugh from his throat, Joel scrubbed his hands around the dog's ears and neck. "He's okay."

"I'm sorry. He must have sensed your distress." Her bottom lip disappeared briefly between her teeth as she offered him an apologetic smile. "Honestly, I could, too."

"I do get stressed thinking about Cici and everything that happened. She had an addiction to opioids. Wish I could have saved her. Wish I'd done a lot of things differently the night I lost her." He was talking to the dog as he continued to pet his warm fur. He was beginning to see how a good therapy dog could truly help someone dealing with tragedy and trauma. A warm, living, breathing distraction. Something to focus on besides stress and pain. "Good boy. Thanks. Go to Mama." Nudging the dog's muscular shoulder, he guided Magnus back to Mollie. "I thought service dogs were supposed to focus on their owner."

"They are. Apparently, I've got the one reject who can't seem to remember that his job is to take care of *me*."

"Shouldn't he be more reliable than that? If he's supposed to protect you?" Maybe he was doing Mollie a disservice by interacting so much with Magnus. But he was smart, all boy, and pretty hard to resist.

"I'm meeting with our trainer tomorrow to see if there's more I can do to make him bond with me. He's deaf in one ear." She explained the flopped-over ear that seemed at odds with the Belgian Malinois's sleek lines. "I wonder if he's losing hearing in the other ear, as well. If he's looking at me and focused on me, he does fine. But he gets distracted too easily."

"I think he's just a friendly guy with a big heart. Trying to help as many people as he can."

"That's not how he's supposed to work."

"Look at how he's rubbing against your hand," Joel pointed out. "He's devoted to you."

"I guess. I'm still taking him in for a refresher course at K-9 Ranch."

"I've heard of the place. Just outside the city." He'd heard the owner had recently married a sheriff's deputy who sometimes helped KCPD with investigations that crossed jurisdictions with the county. "They do good work there. Rescuing dogs. Training them to be companion or service animals."

"I went there looking for a small dog, a little noisemaker who fit my little apartment and could give me the help I needed. But this big guy latched on to me from almost the moment I set foot on the ranch."

"He picked *you*."

"That's what Jessica, the ranch's owner, said, too. Sometimes I think he was just anxious to be adopted, and I was the first sucker to come along who'd take him."

"Don't sell yourself short." He leaned over to pet Magnus again. "This guy's a smart dog. I don't think he'd make a mistake and choose the wrong person."

She rolled her eyes in a *Whatever* retort, and Joel got the idea that Mollie Crane had once been full of wry humor and attitude—before August Di Salvo had beaten the spirit out of her. Parts of his body that hadn't cared about much of anything for a long time perked up at the idea that he could get to know the old Mollie—the real Mollie—if he played his cards right. He was actually excited by the challenge of proving to her that he was someone who was safe enough to be herself with.

With anticipation still sparking through his veins, he stood as Mollie checked her watch and hooked up Magnus's leash. He needed a plan. He needed to spend more time with her. He needed to be the man who could rise to the challenges that A. J. Rodriguez and Mollie herself had unknowingly set before him.

"My break is almost up, and Magnus has done both his businesses," she announced. "I'd better be getting back before Melissa sends out a search party."

Joel helped clean up after the dog. He was racking his brain to come up with something more they could talk about as he held the gate open for an elderly couple bringing a pair of miniature poodles into the dog park. The three dogs sniffed each other as if they were all old friends, and the couple exchanged polite greetings with Mollie. Once she gave the order to *heel*, though, Magnus came right to her side and followed her through the gate. They crossed to the curb and stepped between two parked cars, waiting for the traffic to stop.

Not ready to end their conversation yet, Joel asked, "Melissa is married to a guy I know at KCPD. Sawyer Kincaid?"

Mollie nodded, watching the cars, as well as the pedestrians on either side of the street go by. He was glad to see her be so aware of her surroundings. "He comes in a lot. Sometimes with their kids, sometimes with his partner. He's very protective of her."

He detected the note of wistfulness in her voice and tamped down the urge to be just as protective of Mollie. It wasn't his place. It might never be. "I've seen her at police functions, like the softball game with KCFD."

She smiled, her gaze watching every vehicle that drove past. Gray car. White car. Public works truck. Car with out of state plates. "Yeah. We've got a friendly in-house rivalry at the diner. Melissa is married to a cop, and Corie is married to a firefighter. They've all come in to eat after a game.

They tease each other a lot. I don't always like big, rowdy crowds like that. But it's all in fun. And the tips are great."

He could imagine. "You're more the stay home and read a book or watch a movie on TV kind of gal?"

"I used to enjoy a good celebration. But now I like quiet and predictable, which I guess makes me sound pretty boring, so yes."

Sounded a little bit like undercover work. "Too many people to be on guard against in a crowd, right?"

She looked up at him, perhaps surprised at his understanding, and nodded.

Blue minivan. Gray SUV.

"Still, those softball games are a hell of a lot of fun. You should come watch one." He thumped his thigh. "Not that they're going to ask me to play on the team again anytime soon."

For the first time since he'd known the dog, he heard Magnus growling a low-pitched warning in his throat.

At first, he assumed Magnus was making his presence known to one of the other dogs. But his dark eyes were tracking movement out on the street.

Joel felt his own hackles rise to attention. Black car driving slowly past. Tinted windows. Sunglasses and a lowered sun visor kept the driver's face from being visible. The car flashed its left turn signal and paused at the light. *Yeah, buddy, I notice it, too.*

"Magnus?" Mollie tugged on the dog's leash to turn his attention to her, and the growling ceased. "I don't know what's wrong with him."

"He's protecting you."

"From what?"

Joel was too paranoid to ignore anything suspicious in

the people around him. Maybe if he hadn't ignored the danger signals when he'd run to Cici's aid that night, she'd be alive and he'd still be the cop he once had been. The black car stopped at the traffic light and he instinctively put his hand on Mollie's back and urged her forward. "Let's go."

When she arched her back away from his touch, he quickly pulled away. "I don't mean to flinch every time you touch me."

"My fault," he quickly apologized. "Didn't mean to startle you. Shall we?"

Even without sharing contact, she was moving across the street beside him. "It was good to see you again, Joel."

"Same here." He made sure the car turned the corner and drove away before relaxing enough to continue their conversation. "Is it okay if I stop by again to see you?"

"Why? You've checked up on me." She stopped at the end of the alleyway. "No bruises. No abuser. I'm fine. I don't blame you for anything that happened to me, so you shouldn't blame yourself." She gestured to the cars on the street. "I'm assuming you parked somewhere around here? You don't need to walk me back to the diner."

"Uh-uh. A man makes sure the lady gets safely inside before he leaves her." Especially when the hairs on the back of his neck had been standing on end ever since Magnus had growled.

"Okay, Sir Galahad," she teased. "You may walk me to my alley door."

He fell into step beside her. "While I appreciate you letting me off the hook, I've enjoyed our conversation. I'm fascinated by your dog, curious to know if his training works out. And, I don't want this to come out as an insult—but I feel comfortable with you."

"Why would that be an insult?"

"I should be telling you how pretty you are. That I like your dark hair better than that fake blond look you were sporting two years ago. I should tell you how brave I think you are." He shrugged. "Something more personal and profound than you make me feel comfortable."

"Do you feel comfortable around a lot of other people?"

He pondered her insightful question and gave her an honest answer. "No. Not anymore."

Mollie stopped and tilted her gaze up to his. "Then that was a compliment. And I'll take it as one. Thank you." He saw the whisper of a smile before they walked beside each other once more. "You're welcome to come by the diner anytime. We're a public place, and you can't deny the food is delicious."

"As much as I love the burgers, I actually want to know if I could come to see you."

"Oh. Like a date?"

"Maybe you'd let me take you out to lunch or grab a coffee."

"I'll think about it. I haven't dated anyone since Augie."

They passed one door and then another. "It wouldn't have to be a date. But we could hang out. Talk some more. Be comfortable together."

They were nearing the dumpster behind the diner when she finally nodded. "Okay. But just as friends. And you can't surprise me like you did today. I don't do well with surprises."

"Magnus will save you."

"I'm not holding my breath."

"Give the guy a chance. He might surprise you." Why did that feel like he was trying to sell his own worth, and not the dog's? Joel stopped and pulled out his phone. "Could I have your number? That way I can call or text before I stop by, so it won't be a surprise."

Mollie studied the badge at the middle of his chest, then met his gaze. "I suppose that's the smart thing to do." She pulled out her phone. It was a cheap, pay-by-the-minute style, but it got the job done. "Now text me, so I can program your name and know it's you."

The message he sent was simple and honest. And maybe a little bit hopeful.

You can trust me, Moll.

Her shoulders lifted with a deep sigh. His phone dinged when she texted him back.

I'll try.

Any attempt to confirm that they now qualified as something more than acquaintances fell silent when Magnus barked and lunged forward. "Magnus! What is he doing?" Mollie jerked on his leash. "Magnus. Come."

Oh, he was loving this misfit of a dog. Magnus had sensed the threat even when Joel's guard was down.

The same black car had pulled into the far end of alley. "Do you know that car? Who drives it?"

"No. I—"

"I'm going to take you by the arm now," Joel warned, so Mollie wouldn't be startled. "Get your key out. Walk faster."

Although she quickened her pace and didn't pull away from his hand above her elbow, she still questioned his concern. "Joel, what's wrong?"

"I see that car one time, I don't worry about it. I see it twice, I dismiss it as somebody circling the block because they're lost or looking for a parking space." The windshield reflected the afternoon sun, blinding him to the driver or any passenger inside. "But three times?"

"He's following us?"

The car revved its engine, shifted into gear, and hurtled down the alley toward them. Joel cursed. "Move!"

They ran. But they weren't going to be fast enough. The car nearly clipped a dumpster as it drifted toward their side of the alley.

"Get the door unlocked." He tossed his cane aside, clamped his hands at either side of her waist and lifted her onto the concrete step. While she worked to jam the key into the lock and turn it, he pressed up behind her as the car barreled toward them. "Hurry!"

Magnus nearly tore the leash from her hand as he lunged toward the approaching car. His furious barking echoed off the brick walls like a pack of hounds warning off an intruder.

"Magnus!" Mollie clamped down on the leash to keep the dog from bolting, turning her attention from the door.

"Mollie—lock!"

Leaving the relative safety of the recessed doorway, Joel scooped the dog up in his arms. And with seventy pounds of squirming dog sandwiched between them, he pushed them all forward the second he heard the key turn the lock.

The steel door swung open and the three of them tumbled inside as the heat of the car rushing past swept over them like a crashing wave.

They landed in a tangle of legs and fur on the kitchen floor. He cursed the *oof* of air from Mollie's chest as he landed on top of her. Magnus woofed and scrambled to one side as Joel rolled to the other. When he saw the dog clambering to his feet and heading for the door, he kicked it shut. "Magnus. Stay." He gave the order, having no idea if the dog would obey him or not. "Mollie?"

Joel reached for Mollie to see if she was injured, but she was already pushing herself up to her hands and knees. She glanced over her shoulder, breathing hard, maybe from adrenaline as much as any physical exertion. "Are you all right?"

"Are you?" She'd lost her headband in the fall, and he reached out to push her hair off her face. She snatched his wrist to pull his fingers from her silky curls. "I'm sorry."

"What is going on?" He jumped at the worried female voice above his head. "I heard the commotion at the door and tried to get back here to open it as fast as I could, but... baby belly." Corie Taylor's cheeks blanched as they heard the squeal of brakes and the unmistakable sound of a car jumping the curb and painting rubber across the pavement as it made a sharp turn at high speed. "What is that guy doing? Is he drunk? He could have hit you."

Mollie squeezed Joel's wrist before she pushed him completely away. "Go, if you need to." She turned her head the other way. "Magnus?"

"I got the mutt." Herb had joined the party and had the dog's leash wrapped around his bony fist. "He's fine."

Mollie reached for her dog and wrapped her arms around his neck before nodding to Joel. "Go."

He pushed to his feet, ignoring the twist of pain above his right knee at the sudden movement. He nailed Corie with a look as the pregnant woman leaned over to squeeze Mollie's shoulder. "Stay with her. Make sure she's all right."

He gave the next orders to the Navy vet. "Keep this door locked. I'll knock when I'm ready to come back in."

"Okay. Should I—"

But Joel was already out the door, giving chase, pushing his rebuilt legs as hard as they could go. The car was already out of sight, but he easily followed the tire marks where the car had turned left across traffic. The noise of horns honking and the jumble of cars in the intersection told him the car had cut through a red light. But which way had it gone?

Joel ran to the corner. He held his badge up and stepped between the cars to reach the center of the intersection. He was breathing hard, and the nerves in his right thigh were sparking through his muscles like a shot from a Taser. Joel spun three hundred sixty degrees, looking down every street. But the car had disappeared. The angle had been wrong to even glimpse a license plate number between the parked cars along the sidewalk and uptown traffic.

But he knew cars. And a late-model four-door Lexus RX with tinted windows, gold trim, and a 6-cylinder engine under the hood wasn't one he'd soon forget.

The lights changed and horns honked. He waved an apology to the vehicles that were waiting and jogged back to the sidewalk. He kept his eyes peeled for anything else that pinged his suspicion radar as he hurried back to the diner.

After he checked to make sure Mollie and Magnus were okay, he needed to get to Fourth Precinct headquarters to see if he could get a hit in the system with just a make and a model. He needed to know who was driving that car, and why the driver had been watching Mollie.

Because that "accident" was no accident.

Chapter Five

"Something's wrong with Magnus." Mollie unhooked the dog's harness and sent him off to play with the boy who was tossing balls across the backyard for some of the residents at K-9 Ranch before turning to their training supervisor, Jessica Bennington Caldwell.

The older woman carried two glasses of iced tea across the deck, where it had become their habit to sit for a few minutes and chat after one of Mollie and Magnus's training sessions. Jessica shook her silvering, blond braid down her back and eyed the Belgian Malinois racing ahead of a Black Lab and an Australian shepherd to retrieve the ball. "Wrong? He looks fine to me."

"Penny! Tobes!" The nine-year-old boy called each dog by name and tossed a ball, so each dog had the chance to run and retrieve successfully. Magnus skidded to a stop in the grass and almost knocked the boy down in his enthusiasm for playing the game. "Good boy, Magnus."

"You're doing a good job, Nate," Jessica called out to her foster son. He beamed at the praise and went back to exercising the dogs. Then Jessica handed Mollie one of the glasses and invited her to sit in one of the deck chairs. She leaned down to pet her own service dog, Shadow, a German shepherd mix with a graying muzzle, who seemed content to supervise the activity from his shady spot on the deck, before taking the seat beside her. "Do you think he realizes he's helping me with a chore to earn his allowance?"

Mollie couldn't help but smile at the boy's joyous laughter as he rolled on the ground with the dogs licking his face and silently pleading with Nate to throw the balls again. She looked across the deck to watch Jessie's foster daughter, a sweet blonde girl named Abby, pet and feed treats to a spotted Australian shepherd puppy as she mimicked the training she'd seen Jessie do with the other rescue dogs in her care. "Nate and Abby are two lucky children to have found a home here." She'd heard some of the story of how Jessie had found the two runaway children and taken them in as foster children, and how she had guarded them like a fierce mama bear from a home invasion. "How's the adoption going?"

"We've jumped through all the hoops and filled out more paperwork than you can imagine." Jessie's face softened with a serenely beautiful smile. "But our attorney says they'll be ours before Christmas."

"That's wonderful. Congratulations." Mollie toasted her with her glass. She'd given up on having a family of her own. She had too many hang-ups to manage even a healthy relationship with a man, which she considered a prerequisite to starting a family. But she would dearly love to at least get back into a classroom to surround herself with young people again. If only she didn't have the specter of the Di Salvo family hanging over her. "I have to admit I'm a little jealous. You have this beautiful property, your amazing dogs, two children to love—and let's not forget the hunky deputy sheriff you married last month."

"You ladies talking about me out here?" The back door opened again and a tall, well-built man wearing a sheriff's department uniform walked out. Garrett Caldwell pulled a departmental ball cap off his spiky salt-and-pepper hair and leaned down to trade a kiss with Jessie. Then another one. Mollie politely looked away from the love shining between them.

"You're home early." Jessie's tone was happy, but her expression looked vaguely worried.

"Relax. Nothing's wrong." He pressed his thumb against the dimple of his wife's frown to ease her concern. "The county is relatively quiet today. I'm the boss of my department, so I decided to grant myself permission to spend an extra hour with my beautiful family." Mollie looked back as Jessie's husband straightened and pulled the tea from his wife's hand to steal a long swallow. "Mollie. How are you doing today?"

"I'm fine."

Garrett dropped his gaze to Jessie and the two exchanged a look. He handed off the sweating glass and put his cap back on his head. "I'll keep an eye on the kids. Looks like you two were in the middle of an important conversation."

"Thanks, sweetheart."

He winked a goodbye to Mollie, then headed over to Abby to scoop the giggling little girl up in his arms. He carried her down to the grass where he traded a fist bump with Nate and listened patiently as both children recounted the highlights of their day.

Jessie had inherited the seven-acre property that had once been a working farm and converted it into a dog training facility, as well as a spacious country home, allowing them the distance they needed to share a private conversation. "So…" Jessie sipped her tea. "You don't think Magnus is working out as service dog? I thought your training session went well today. Especially with the nonverbal cues. His reactions to you were spot-on."

Mollie nodded. It was hard to explain the difference in Magnus's behavior when he was here on the ranch to when he was with her in the city. She didn't want her boy to be labeled a failure any more than she wanted to feel like one when it came to their working relationship. "Do I need to get his hearing tested again? He doesn't always seem to be aware when I need him unless he's looking right at me."

"And…?"

"And what?"

"He's barely two years old. Just out of his puppyhood. Maybe it's taking him longer to mature, but I don't think so." Jessie turned her head to point out how responsive Magnus was to Nate's commands as he showed off his skills for his foster dad. "He's a clown, but he can also turn on work mode faster than any dog here. He wants to work. He wants to have a job and do it well. He wants to please you."

Mollie reached down into her bag beside her, where she'd hidden Magnus's toy. "What he wants is his teddy bear."

Jessie laughed. "That, too. He's definitely more reward driven than treat driven." The older woman set her glass on the table between them and leaned a little closer. "We can take Magnus to my vet again, if you think his hearing loss is a legitimate concern. But we already knew he was going to be more responsive to visual cues. Is he not answering your verbal commands when you're away from the ranch?"

"He went to this guy I was talking to yesterday and put his paws on him. Laid his head on his lap just like he does with me." Mollie wasn't sure if she was explaining her hit-

or-miss success with Magnus clearly enough so that the other woman would understand her fears. "*I* was stressing because I don't always handle social situations that well anymore. I was sitting right there, and he ignored me. He's supposed to be *my* dog, and he went and comforted someone else."

"Was this a one-on-one situation, or something with more people, like the diner when there's a run of customers?"

"I was exercising Magnus. He asked if he could go with me to talk. It was the two of us and the dog."

"Hmm... Maybe you weren't as panicked about being with *this guy* as you thought you were. Maybe there's something about *this guy* and having Magnus with you that made you comfortable enough to be with him."

Comfortable. There was that word again. Joel said he felt comfortable with her. But did she feel the same? Joel was a man—an attractive one at that, if a little beat up around the edges. And he knew about her time with Augie. How could she possibly feel comfortable with a man connected to the past she could never truly move on from?

Jessie's gray eyes narrowed as she pondered Mollie's story. She glanced out into the yard to see the three panting dogs sitting in front of Garrett and the children, eagerly waiting for the balls to go flying again. Magnus's razor-sharp focus was impossible to miss. Once the dogs took off, Jessie looked over at Mollie, nodding as if she had some kind of answer for her. "Was *this guy* in distress? Could he have been having a panic attack like you do sometimes?"

It was Mollie's turn to carefully think over her response. She'd asked Joel about his injuries, but he'd skimmed the details, either protecting her sensibilities or protecting himself from reliving a painful memory. He'd made a joke, but his knuckles were white where he gripped his cane. And then he'd mentioned his girlfriend dying. His tone had sounded so bleak. His golden-brown eyes had seemed so distant. And she thought he was going to snap that cane in two. That was when Magnus had targeted him. She'd had the urge to comfort him, too. If she was a toucher, she would have squeezed his hand or offered him a hug. But Magnus had stepped up and done what she hadn't been willing to do. "Yes. He was very stressed at the moment."

"It's rare for a service dog to respond to anyone but the human he's bonded with. Maybe our boy here is so smart, he responds to anyone in distress. My Shadow does that with the kids." Mollie sat up a little straighter, watching her dog with a sense of pride. Maybe there wasn't anything wrong with Magnus. Maybe her boy was smarter than she'd given him credit for. "Is there a personal connection between you and this *guy*?"

Surprised by the question, Mollie swung her gaze back to her friend. "Personal? With Joel?"

"Joel. Okay, at least I don't have to keep calling him *this guy*." Jessie smiled. "This Joel—have you been dating him? He's not your brother or a family friend, is he?"

"I don't have any family."

"So, you are dating?" Jessie continued before she could correct the misassumption. "Magnus may see you as a family unit, and he's responding to you both because he wants to protect his entire pack."

"I'm not dating him," Mollie blurted out. "I sat and had a conversation with him for fifteen minutes. Sure, we discussed some surprisingly deep stuff, but that's just where the conversation went. I've met him a couple of times before, and he was always nice to me. He doesn't look nice—I mean, he looks more like a thug or a street fighter or something dangerous like that. I think he must look that way for his work. But he was always nice to me."

Picking up on her rambling discomfort, Jessie reached across the table to touch the arm of the chair, where Mollie squeezed her fist. "I'm not your therapist—I rehabilitate dogs, not people. But it sounds like you have feelings for him."

Did she? How could she?

"I…I guess we share a connection." She vividly remembered Joel tackling her and Magnus when that car had nearly run them down. And when he'd come back after chasing the car, he'd come right up to Mollie to make sure she was all right before he called the near hit-and-run in to someone at KCPD. He apologized for the bruises on her knees, even though she assured him they were quite minor compared to the injuries she could have sustained if that car had hit them. As frightened as she'd been of that car racing toward them, she hadn't completely shut down in panic when he'd lifted her to safety and shoved her and Magnus into the kitchen ahead of him. Then she'd given him her phone number because he'd revealed some things that made her think he was just as broken as she was, and, like her, was trying to move on with his life and find his new normal. "I *am* comfortable with him. Yes."

He'd said those words about her, and now she was saying them about Joel. They both had a lot of emotional baggage to deal with, but it hadn't seemed to matter when they'd sat down and talked. It had all felt so normal, and she hadn't shared anything *normal* with a man for a very long time.

Jessie patted her hand before pulling back. "I'm not trying to put you on the spot, but I do need to understand what's happening so that I can evaluate Magnus's behavior and figure how to retrain him. Or if it's truly necessary."

"That makes sense." She thought she understood the point Jessie was making, even if she didn't find it completely reassuring. "Magnus protects my world. And if someone is part of that world, then Magnus thinks he has to protect that person, too?" Jessie nodded. "But Joel and I are friends. Barely that. I need Magnus to be there for *me*, not everyone else."

Jessie stood and crossed to the deck railing to watch the dogs interacting with her husband and foster children more closely. "Can you ask Joel to come to a training session with you? I'd like to observe the three of you together. Then I could tell if Magnus is switching loyalties, or if he's just being a typical Mal—" Jessie's nickname for the Belgian Malinois dogs she worked with "—who's looking for a bigger, more demanding job to do."

"You want me to invite Joel here?" Mollie wiped the icy condensation from her glass, then palmed the back of her neck beneath her hair to cool her skin. The late afternoon was hot with the sun high in the hazy blue sky. But it was the mix of nervous anticipation and a familiar dread at purposely developing a relationship with a man that made her temperature spike.

"Yes. If you're nervous about it, just remember that I'll be with you the whole time. Do you feel safe with Joel? I can make sure Garrett is home when you're here." Jessie turned to face Mollie, leaning her hips against the railing. "The kids will be here, of course, since they're off for the summer from school. That reminds me. Have you given any more thought to tutoring Nate on his math skills? He qualified for the HAL program in math. But since this is a new school, I don't want him to feel like he's out of sync with the other students when he starts fourth grade this year."

Mollie finally set down her glass and joined Jessie at the railing. "Sure. I'd love to repay you by helping him with math. I miss working with students."

"Good. Then I'll see you, Joel, and Magnus tomorrow. If that time still works for you?"

Mollie tried not to feel like she was being rushed into this. Impulsive behavior had been smacked out of her by Augie years ago. And the secrets she'd kept since her divorce demanded she be cautious about her dealings with people. "I'll have to check with Joel to see if his schedule allows him to get away in the afternoon."

Reaching over, Jessie squeezed her hand where she clutched the railing. "Make it happen. It's as important for Magnus as it is for you that we get this problem straightened out. Some dogs can't be trained to be more than the family pet. And that's okay. Being the family pet is an important job. But I've never met a Mal who couldn't be trained to do more. Even without his hearing, he's a high-energy dog. We need to focus that energy, or he could become difficult to control. Might even become dangerous to himself or to others."

Mollie pictured Magnus going after that black car yesterday in the alley behind the diner. No one on the outside needed to know that her dog was a happy boy who loved his teddy bear and a good tummy rub. He looked and sounded dangerous when he perceived a threat to her.

Augie had always driven black cars. For a brief moment in that alley yesterday, her stomach had bottomed out at the idea that not only had he tracked her down—a nightmare she'd suspected would eventually happen—but he'd violated one of the few details of their divorce agreement by getting close to her again and threatening her.

Of course, the dangerous driver in the alley could have been a drunk driver. Maybe he thought he was still on one of the main streets. Or maybe the impatient driver had taken a shortcut and driven so fast the car had been nearly out of control.

Augie had always been an impatient driver.

Even before that first time he'd assaulted her, she'd seen glimpses of road rage when he was driving. She should have gotten a clue about his selfish, irrational, violent behavior long before that Thanksgiving night. His mother, Bernadette, had insisted he use a driver on staff as often as possible to protect the heir to the Di Salvo fortune—keeping Augie from behind the wheel in order to keep his name out of traffic court records and keep him in one piece.

A staff driver reminded her of Joel and the few months he'd worked for the family. Although he'd been at the periphery of her world, other than that first night they'd met, she'd sensed even then that he was a good man. Someone she should be able to trust. Someone who wanted to keep her safe.

He seemed a harder version of that good man now. Something about the accident he'd glossed over, as well as the girlfriend he'd lost to drugs had changed him. Not just the limp or the visible scars—but the scars on the inside. Oh, he was still very much a protector. The way he'd shoved both her and Magnus out of the path of that reckless driver, then run off to see if he could identify the man, proved that.

But was he still the man who'd spoken so gently to her, who'd tempted her to lean into his strength and allow someone stronger to stand between her and Augie? Mollie had sensed the reticence in him today. Maybe it was sorrow or guilt. Self-doubts that he'd failed the woman he'd loved. He'd been dealing with a lot of emotional stress. Clearly, Magnus had picked up on that, too.

"Mollie?" Jessica touched her arm. She startled but didn't shy away.

Magnus was staring at her from the middle of the yard, and when she made eye contact, he trotted up the steps to push his head into her hand and lean against her thigh. Mollie instantly breathed easier at the warm contact. She scratched around his ears and knew he'd become much more than her service dog. Maybe that was why she was honestly afraid that his loyalty wasn't to her. She had no one in her life beyond a few work friends and this dog. She needed someone or something to belong to her—someone who wanted her to belong to them, too. "Good boy. You're my good boy."

"You were a million miles away." Jessie asked permission before she petted and praised Magnus, too. "I don't think you need to worry about Magnus being your dog. But I still think it would be a good idea to bring your Joel to a training session tomorrow."

Her Joel?

She hadn't thought she could do a relationship again. So why wasn't she correcting Jessie's assumption about her friendship with Detective Standage?

"I'll talk to him. I really want Magnus to work out as my service dog. I… I'm getting attached to this big goof."

"I'm glad to hear that. Come on. Let's run him through one more set of commands before you head back to the city.

Hook him to his leash, and we'll go out to the barn, away from the distractions of playing children."

They went through one more session of basic dog commands, using both verbal and visual cues. Then there was another round of pets from Nate, a shy hug from Abby, and Mollie had a worn-out Magnus loaded into the back seat of her car where he stretched out on his blanket and cuddled with his teddy bear while she pulled out her cell phone.

She waved to Jessie and her family and held up her phone to show them she'd be sitting in their driveway for a few minutes while she contacted Joel.

Mollie stared at the blank screen of her phone for a full minute, working up the courage to text Joel. She hadn't purposely contacted a man for several months now.

When she heard a whine from the back seat, she lifted her gaze to the rearview mirror and saw that Magnus had raised his head to look at her, tilting his head as if to ask if she needed him. Mollie smiled, then reached back to pet him. "I sat here too long without speaking or moving, didn't I? I didn't mean to worry you." When she reached his flank, he stretched out and gave her full access to a tummy rub. "You're mama's good boy. You go ahead and rest now. You've earned a break."

When she faced the steering wheel again, she breathed out a determined sigh. She could do this for Magnus. She fingered her locket, summoning the confident young woman her granny had raised. Then she pulled up Joel's number. With only a few numbers on her phone, it was easy to find. She typed before self-doubts and second-guessing could get in her head again.

Hey, Joel. Is this a good time?

Only a few seconds passed before he answered.

For what? Miss my scintillating charm already?

Are you still at work? I can text you later if you're busy.

Sorry. Ignore my sarcasm. I try to be funny when I get nervous.

Why would you be nervous?

Because a pretty woman I like just texted me.

Mollie glanced at her reflection in the rearview mirror. Her hair was a windswept mess from spending the past two hours outside. Her cheeks were flushed from the sun, and the only makeup she had on was some pink gloss to protect her lips. Shorts, sneakers, and a faded Worlds of Fun T-shirt she hadn't even bothered to tuck in completed her look. She was a far cry from the perfect beauty Augie had demanded she be.

So why did Joel Standage saying she was pretty make her smile when Augie's praise had only made her feel trapped and on edge?

His three blinking dots turned into a message before she could answer.

I'm not taking it back. You're pretty. I like you. And you texted me. You can't argue with that logic.

I don't know what to say to that.

You don't have to say anything. Things are winding down here on my shift. This is a perfect time to chat. What's up?

She glanced back at Magnus. Her boy had fallen asleep already, with his muzzle lying on top of his bear. Poor guy had put in a full day. She needed to take care of him.

I need to ask you a favor.

Clearly, he'd been texting while he waited for her response.

I didn't have a LP# to ID the owner of the car that played chicken with us yesterday. But I did find out that Edward Di Salvo and your ex both own that make of car.

LP# must mean License Plate number. Sure, she could go off on a tangent with him. Besides, she'd already suspected that yesterday's incident had something to do with Augie. Confirming her worst fear or having another rational explanation for nearly being run down would at least tell her what she was dealing with.

Augie always valued what his parents said. If Edward said that was the kind of car someone of their station would own, then Augie would get one, too.

Sadly, they aren't the only drivers in the state who own that make of car. I can't even say for sure it belongs to a K.C. resident.

So, you're saying it's not much of a lead.

It's not even enough to get a warrant to look at their cars to see if they have the kind of scratches and alignment issues it would have sustained from jumping curbs and turning at the speed that guy was going.

Mollie shook her head. She really wanted it to be a drunk driver. She might not be able to identify who was behind the wheel yesterday, but she had a feeling she knew who'd sent him.

What's the favor? You can ask me anything.

Right. She didn't really want to be talking about the Di Salvos right now, either. She typed in her request.

Would you be willing to come to a training session with me and Magnus tomorrow at K-9 Ranch?

Yes.

She huffed a sound that was almost a laugh at his easy acquiescence.

Don't you want to know what time? Or why I need you?

I enjoyed our time together yesterday. Before someone tried to run us down. My schedule is flexible, so I'll make it work. You need me? I'm there.

Magnus is the one who needs you.

I'm still in. You two are a package deal. Besides, I like the guy. Wait. Is he okay?

He's snoring in my back seat right now.

:) Go Magnus. Play hard and sleep well.

Jessie—our trainer—wants to see how Magnus interacts differently when you're around. Why he doesn't focus on me when you're there.

He's your dog, Moll. I'm sorry if I screwed up his training.

It might be nothing. Maybe you're a distraction. Maybe he's creating his own job. Jessie can't help me until she sees the three of us together.

What time?

4 p.m.?

Yes. Do we drive together? Should I pick you up someplace? Work? Your apartment?

I don't know if I'm comfortable being alone in a car with you. It's not you. It's my own hang-up.

Augie hadn't even let her drive after the first few months of their marriage. She'd thought it was sweet at first, that he was taking care of her. But she eventually realized he was controlling where she went, and making sure she was never alone. And the punishment he meted out hadn't been limited to the closed doors of the estate, either. Being trapped in the back seat of a car with Augie wasn't an experience she cared to remember.

Her phone dinged, dragging her out of her thoughts.

I'm not your ex. But I can drive separately.

Making even a simple decision like sharing a ride had been taken out of her hands when she'd been Mollie Di Salvo. No more.

I don't want to be paranoid for the rest of my life.

I don't want you to be afraid of me. Ever. If that means you don't want to be shut up in a vehicle with me, that's what we'll do. I'll drive my truck and meet you there.

No. She was braver than this. Granny Crane would be pointing a stern finger at her right now if she let Joel think she was afraid of him, specifically. Inhaling deeply, she typed away.

Change of plans. Would you mind driving the three of us? I don't think we'd all fit in my compact car very comfortably.

You sure?

Yes. She could do terse and direct, too.

Magnus can sit in the seat between us.

Deal. She texted him her address. Just pull up in front of

the building. We'll be waiting in the lobby and will come out when we see you. We'll need twenty minutes to get there.

I'll be there. Red pickup truck. It doesn't look like much on the outside, but she's a peach on the inside.

Sounded a little like Joel himself.

While she was smiling at that revelation, the surprisingly chatty detective texted her a new message.

See you tomorrow at 4. Thanks for asking me. It means a lot to me that you want me to help.

It means a lot to me that you said yes.

Are you driving?

Not yet. I'm still at K-9 Ranch.

Put your phone down and get yourself safely home. I'll see you tomorrow around 3:30.

See you then.

As if he knew she was still looking at her screen, savoring their rambling conversation, another text from Joel popped up.

Phone down. Drive safely. See you tomorrow.

Bossy much?

You have no idea.

Before she gave in to her curiosity to ask him to explain that response, Mollie stuck her phone into the cup holder between the seats and started her car. She replayed their conversation in her head as she drove down Highway 40, heading into Kansas City. She smiled when she realized that had been the longest conversation she'd had with a man in ages. Yeah, they'd covered some serious stuff, but they'd been silly, too. It felt good. And normal.

She liked normal.

She liked Joel, too.

She was still smiling as she parked her car in the private lot behind her building. She gave Magnus a few minutes in the grassy median, then they ran up the stairs to her second-floor apartment.

That's when the smiling stopped.

Mollie froze at the top of the stairs, pulling Magnus to a halt beside her. There was a newspaper tacked to her door— the weekend society page from the *Kansas City Journal*, with a picture and headline announcing the engagement of August Di Salvo to a woman she recognized, one of the family's attorneys and his longtime mistress, Kyra Schmidt. Kyra looked as blonde and beautiful and dressed to highbrow perfection as she'd once done for Augie.

But seeing her ex's face on her front door wasn't the thing that made her blood run cold. It was the message scrawled across the paper in black marker.

You know what I want. Make this right. Don't ruin this for me.

The door itself wasn't quite shut. She could tell by the scratches on the lock that it had been jimmied open. "Magnus, sit. Stay." Avoiding both the newspaper and the knob, she nudged it open with her elbow. The old, walnut-stained wood door creaked open to reveal careless destruction. "Oh, God."

Her apartment was small. The only interior doors were a closet and a bathroom. But they both stood open. The mattress where she slept had been flipped off the bed, the pillows cut open. And every drawer and cabinet were open or overturned on the floor. Even Magnus's bed had been torn open, its stuffing strewn about like cotton candy.

She heard Magnus whining beside her and looked down to find his nose tilted up to her. Right. Stay in the moment. Freezing up in panic wouldn't do her any good. She bent down to pet the Belgian Malinois around the head before patting his flank and pulling him away. "Magnus, with me."

Mollie instinctively touched her locket through her T-shirt as she retreated. When her back hit the opposite wall, she yanked the chain from beneath her shirt and opened the locket. She breathed out a sigh of relief when she saw the tiny, folded piece of paper opposite her granny's picture inside. Then she reached down and fingered the small pocket in Magnus's harness, nodding when she felt the small object hidden there. "Good boy. Good boy, Magnus."

She knew what the intruder was looking for. He'd never get his hands on it as long as she was alive. Keeping it well hidden and out of Augie's reach was the only thing *keeping* her alive.

Make this right? As if. August Di Salvo was never getting his hands on it. It was the only bargaining chip she had.

Why was this happening now? What had changed in Augie's world to prompt him to come after her like this?

His engagement? While she pitied Kyra for saying yes to his proposal, Mollie was more than happy to see him move on to another woman and leave any connection with her behind. This had to be related to the car that tried to kill them yesterday. Or maybe the goal was to scare her. Or make her retreat so far into her fear that she'd be an easy mark for someone to complete the job.

But he wasn't getting his hands on what she'd taken from her ex-husband. It was the only leverage she'd had to get away from him, to get his signature on the divorce papers, to keep him from hurting her ever again. Augie didn't get to win this time.

She was deep into her mental pep talk when she heard the clanging of a ring of keys and an old metal toolbox coming down the stairs from the third floor. "What the…?"

Mollie cringed at the building manager's reaction to her door. She yelped when Mr. Williams swung around to face her.

"You okay, Miss Crane? Looks like somebody busted in." He set down his toolbox and moved closer to the door, inspecting the same damage she had. "I've been upstairs all afternoon working on that broken pipe between 304 and 305. I never heard a thing."

He scratched the back of his thinning gray hair. "How'd they get inside the building without one of the residents' key fobs?"

"Don't touch anything!" she warned, shaking herself out of her terrified stupor. "There may be evidence."

"You're right, ma'am. Goll-darnit." He unrolled the sleeve of his gray coveralls to cover his fingers before pulling the door closed again. "They busted my lock." Right.

Because that was the worst of what had happened here today. "Good thing you weren't home, Miss... Miss Crane?"

Mollie was already charging down the stairs, swiping away the tears that threatened to fall so she could dig her phone out of her back pocket and pull up a familiar name. When she reached the bottom step, she perched on the edge of it and typed.

Joel? I need a cop.

She stared intently at the screen, waiting for his response. Then she startled so badly when her cell rang that she dropped her phone. She quickly scrambled to pick it up from between her feet, sending up a silent prayer of thanks when she read the name and answered. "Joel?"

"What's wrong?" His gruff voice didn't sound at all like the jokester she'd been texting a half hour earlier. She threw her arm around Magnus's shoulders and reminded herself of the decision she'd made during that conversation. Joel Standage was a good man. Beat up by life and rough around the edges, but he made her smile, he liked her dog, and he made her feel safe. "Mollie?"

"I'm here."

Joel cursed. "Don't scare me like that. Where are you? Are you hurt? Are you in danger?"

She answered each question as quickly as he'd rattled them off. "My apartment building. No. I'm not sure."

"I'm on my way to you now. Tell me what's going on."

"He broke into my apartment."

"He? Di Salvo? Is he still there?"

"I don't think so." She heard a siren in the background of the call. Joel must have one of those portable models he stuck on the roof of his vehicle. "Augie or someone who works for him was here. They left a message, and it looks like they went through the whole place. I don't have much, but I think everything has been touched."

"Do you have something he wants?"

She glanced around the empty foyer and tuned out the voices in the hallway above her as Mr. Williams knocked on doors and asked the other residents if they'd had a break-in, too. She knew the answer was no. This wasn't a break-in. It was a targeted search. After nearly a year of so-called freedom, Augie was coming after her.

"Mollie?"

"Yes. I have something. He…he didn't find it. I didn't hide it in my apartment." She could hear a siren close by now. A black-and-white pulled up out front, sliding into the fifteen-minute loading zone at the curb. She didn't think detectives drove squad cars. "What are you driving?"

"My truck. Red pickup."

"Did you call for backup? There's already a police car here."

Mr. Williams and his rattling toolbox came down the stairs. "*I* called them. I read that heinous message on your door." He leaned over to pat her back or squeeze her shoulder, but Magnus put himself between her and the super and growled.

"Magnus!" She tugged him back to her side.

Mr. Williams gave them a wide berth as he stepped down to the foyer. "That dog's a menace. When I said you could have a pet, I didn't mean an attack dog."

"He can tell I'm scared. He's protecting me. You may have startled him because that's the side he can't hear on.

He won't hurt you unless I tell him to." At least, she hoped he was that disciplined of a dog.

Joel's voice shouted in her ear. "Who's that? Who are you talking to?"

"The building super. He called 9-1-1."

"Don't talk to anyone until I get there. I'm only a few minutes away."

When she saw the two uniformed officers getting out of the car, she gasped and pulled her knees to her chest, instinctively folding herself into a smaller presence. "Joel?"

"Right here, babe."

"Remember that police officer who wouldn't keep his hands to himself at the diner last October?"

"Yeah. Rocky Garner. What about him?"

"He's here."

Joel swore again. "Do not talk to him. Magnus with you?"

"Yes."

"Good. Keep him between you and Garner."

"Okay."

"I'm in your neighborhood now. I'll be there shortly. You're going to be okay, Moll. You're stronger than Augie. You survived him. You'll survive this, too."

"You have a lot of faith in me."

"Hell, yeah, I do."

She took a deep breath at his words and pulled her shoulders back. "Don't get hurt driving over here. I'm okay."

"Damn right, you are."

She almost smiled. "You know, Joel, you cuss a lot when you're fired up."

"That going to be a problem for you?" Did that mean he was an emotional hothead? She wasn't a big fan if that was the case. Or was the problem that he intended to be around her more often?

She hoped it was the latter. "As long as you're not cussing at me."

"Never."

She watched Rocky Garner and his partner climb the front steps to the building. The handsy officer adjusted his protective vest, his gun, and his hat before he made eye contact with her through the glass. Then he smiled. He remembered her, too.

Mollie shivered. "Joel?"

"Yeah, babe?"

"Hurry."

Chapter Six

There wasn't a ball small enough Mollie could curl into. Officer Rocky Garner removed his hat and made a beeline toward her spot on the bottom step. "You the one who had the break-in, sweetheart? Are you okay? You're not hurt, are you?"

The words were right, but the person saying them, and the slick way they were said, was wrong.

Mr. Williams stepped in front of Rocky before he could reach her. "I'm the one who called it in, Officer. We don't get a lot of break-ins here, but this one's serious."

Officer Garner seemed confused, then displeased, to have the gray-haired man impede his progress toward Mollie. But he pasted a smile on his face before patting the man's shoulder. "You the manager here?"

"Yes, sir."

"Fine. That's just fine." Officer Garner stepped back and gestured to the Black officer, who appeared to be his partner. "Why don't you give your statement to Darnell there, and I'm going to talk to the victim."

"I dunno. Miss Crane is a little shaken up. She knows me. I could stay…" Mr. Williams glanced back at her, then seemed to think better of going against Garner's suggestion and left Mollie to fend for herself.

"She's in good hands with me." The smarmy officer assured her super before propping his elbows on his holster and utility belt and facing her with a deceptively casual stance. "Mollie, isn't it? You're a mite prettier out of uniform. Sorry this happened to you. Want to show me your apartment where the break-in happened?"

She glanced out the glass doors at the front of the lobby, hoping Joel would make a miraculous entrance and save her from having to talk to Rocky Garner. But no such luck. The street was in the throes of rush hour traffic, and there was no place to park on either side. If he parked in the back of the building, he'd have to knock hard and flash his badge to get someone to let him in. If that didn't happen, he'd have to run around to the front, where Mr. Williams or one of her curious neighbors who were gathering to see what the police being there was all about, could admit him.

But no red pickup. No Joel. No miracle.

"Ma'am? Let's go." Any deception about casual or friendly disappeared when he leaned toward her and latched his fingers against her elbow. "You on the main floor or upstairs?"

Mollie jerked her arm, but couldn't immediately break his grasp. At the same time she breathed in his coffee and mint-scented breath, Magnus growled, low in his throat.

Officer Garner released her and held both hands up in mock surrender. "Your mutt has a mean streak in him. I'm afraid you're going to have to muzzle him or lock him in a neighbor's bathroom, so I can walk through the crime scene with you."

Mollie shook her head. "He stays with me. Always."

"Bet that puts a damper on your love life, don't it?" He snickered at his own joke.

"Please don't touch me again, Officer. I have panic attacks. I do better when the dog is with me."

His dark eyes narrowed at her attempt to stand up for herself. "You a mental case?"

She cringed at his crass comments. Either he thought he was being funny and was woefully mistaken about his level of charm or he was legitimately one of the biggest jerks she'd ever met. And that was saying something.

Anger surged ahead of her fear, and Mollie pushed to her feet, holding Magnus's leash tightly in her hands. "Are you married, Officer Garner?"

"Nope. Divorced twice."

"I can see why," she muttered under her breath, ducking her head.

"Excuse me?"

"I said this way," she answered in a stronger voice. With his blatant innuendos and touchy-feely hands, it didn't surprise her that marriage wasn't a strength of his. But she kept her comments to herself and headed up the stairs. "My apartment is on the second floor."

She felt the officer's gaze like laser beams on her backside as he followed her to the second floor. "Why'd you ask? You interested? You always seem like such a prickly thing at Pearl's. But I'm willing to try anything once."

Her granny would have slapped the man's face by now and lectured him up one side and down the other. Mollie was sorely tempted to do the same. Instead, she kept her cool and pointed out her front door before stepping aside and putting Magnus in a sit between her and the police officer. "That's my place."

He let out a long, low whistle before pulling his phone out and snapping a few pictures of the newspaper and threat.

"Make *what* right? You know this Di Salvo dude? Looks like he's pretty pissed at you. Why would he threaten you?"

Threaten? Mollie blinked back the images that tried to sneak out of her memories. Hair literally pulled from her scalp. Vile words. A punch to the mouth if she dared to talk back.

The memories blended with the commotion down in the lobby, her neighbors whispering in the doorways, and Officer Garner pushing open her door. "Boy, he sure did a number on your place." He snapped a few more pictures. "You're lucky you weren't here. What did he take?"

Magnus was leaning against her leg and pushing his cold nose into her hand when she heard footsteps on the stairs and turned with an audible sigh of relief at the sight of Joel's muscular shoulders and golden-brown eyes. Magnus's tail thumped the floor with a similar anticipation. "Joel."

"You two okay?" were the first words out of his mouth. He crossed straight to her, his limp barely slowing his stride. For a second, she thought he was going to touch her face or hair with his outstretched hand. But at the last moment, he reached down and scrubbed Magnus around his ears. "Good boy. You keeping Mama safe?"

She wondered what his fingertips would feel like against her skin, and she acknowledged a moment of envy that he'd petted her dog instead. But she was beyond happy to see him here and felt herself take a normal breath under his watchful eyes. "We're fine." She glanced around at the neighbors peeking from their open doors before nodding to Rocky Garner and the officer talking to the super and more residents downstairs. "It got crowded pretty fast."

"And you don't like crowds." He raised the badge hanging from the lanyard around his neck and flashed it to the other residents. "I'm Detective Standage, KCPD. I need you all to go back to your apartments and lock your doors." He might look like he'd just climbed off a Harley with his tattoos and beard stubble, but he spoke with an authority that got the others moving from being curious onlookers to respecting her privacy. "Everything is fine. Miss Crane and her dog are safe and so are all of you. Thank you for your cooperation." He dropped his warm brown gaze back to her as the others did as he requested. "I didn't lie to them, did I?"

Mollie shook her head. "I'm okay. Magnus is, too. He's been great." She dropped her voice to a whisper. "He growled at Officer Garner when he tried to take my arm."

Joel grinned and reached down to give Magnus the praise he loved. "Good dog."

He gave her a nod before turning to the uniformed police officer standing in her open doorway. "What are you doing here, Garner?"

"What are *you* doing here? I answered a call from Dispatch about a B&E."

Joel looked beyond him to the open door and muttered a low curse. "And making terroristic threats. That's clearly a personal message on her door."

"Whatever. You may be schtooping the victim, but this is *my* call."

Joel moved toward the bigger man. "Watch your mouth, Garner."

"Butt out, you has-been."

"You're a patrol officer, not an investigator. Do. Your. Job."

Rocky Garner was a good four of five inches taller than Joel, and he was squaring off as if he was looking for a fight. "I will be an investigator. I'm the one who's up for a promotion in two months. You're on your way out."

Mollie moved up behind Joel and brushed her fingers against the fist at his side, not wanting to be a part of any more violence today. She gasped when Joel's fist opened, and he laced his fingers together with hers and clasped her hand firmly in his, keeping her behind him out of Garner's line of sight, but maintaining the connection. Instead of panicking or pulling away, she followed her first instinct and tightened her grip in his.

"Your job is to secure and control the scene, calling for whatever backup you need. Not to go all cowboy and stomp all over the crime scene yourself. Be smart, man. You had at least seven witnesses on the scene besides Miss Crane. Do you know their names? Their locations? Did they see or hear anything? Are any of them traumatized by what happened here? Are they suspects?"

"Are you calling me stupid?" Mollie's breathing rate increased right along with Officer Garner's. He turned red in the face as his anger consumed him. "Telling me I don't know how to do my job?"

"I'm trying to keep the peace here, which is what you should be doing. Not upsetting people." Joel remained surprisingly calm, which made her feel better, but only seemed to aggravate the uniformed officer. "Especially not Miss Crane."

"I heard about you, Standage," Garner taunted. "How you blew your last assignment. People died."

Joel's grip pulsed around hers.

Uh-uh. She wasn't letting this man denigrate Joel or make her nervous any longer. She threaded Magnus's leash through the belt loop on her jeans and tapped 9-1-1 on her phone.

When the Dispatcher answered, she apologized for not knowing exactly who to call and gave the woman her name and address. "Yes, ma'am. There's a police officer who's arguing with a detective. I think he's trying to start a fight."

"Mollie…" She wasn't sure if Joel was warning her he didn't need her help, or if she was making things worse.

But she identified the threat when asked and read the badge number off Rocky Garner's chest. "I'm the victim whose apartment was broken into, and he's saying crude things about me. It's not the first time he's harassed me. Who can I report this to?"

Officer Garner broke his stare-down with Joel and nailed her with an accusatory glare. "Who are you talking to, lady?"

"9-1-1. They're giving me the number to call to file a complaint." Joel squeezed her hand, hopefully applauding her initiative in making the call.

"A complaint? Screw you, lady. I came here to help you. It looks like you've got some bad juju headed your way, and I put my life on the line to protect you. You should be grateful I answered the call." He shoved Joel away, cursed as Magnus shifted to his feet and growled, and headed down the stairs to the lobby. "C'mon, Darnell. We'll wait outside and let the mighty detective handle the hysterical female."

They both watched until Officer Garner stormed out the front door. His partner made some sort of apology to Mr. Williams before heading out after him.

"I'm not hysterical," Mollie whispered. "I'm pissed off." She raised her voice to a more normal tone and called after the retreating cop. "And who says 'bad juju' anymore, anyway?" She practically growled herself as her emotions surged through her. "He's so old-school. And not in a good way."

"There's a good way?"

"Yes. Chivalry and kindness. Not, men rule the world and women are their minions to do with and talk to as they please—and then expect us to be grateful for that kind of attention."

"I'll take angry over scared any day." Joel chuckled and held his hand out for her phone. "May I?"

"Oh." She felt her cheeks heat with embarrassment. "I forgot she was still on the line. Sorry."

Mollie handed it over and Joel took over the call, giving the Dispatcher his own badge number and explaining the situation. "The threat has been neutralized," he assured her. "A disagreement on jurisdiction. I've already called in for backup. I appreciate your help in calming my witness. Yes, ma'am. I think she's going to be just fine." His gaze remained locked on hers the entire conversation, reassuring her that, despite Garner's taunts and her outburst, he did, indeed, have the situation under control. "You bet."

Joel ended the call, and she tucked her phone back into her pocket. "Did I overstep?" she asked. "Make things worse for you?"

"For me? Hell, no. I hate the way Garner talks to you. To any female from what I've heard. I'm guessing the sensitivity training we all have taken hasn't rubbed off on him yet."

"I guess not." She huffed out a relieved breath that the officer had gone.

"That was cool to see you stand up to him."

Mollie shook off the compliment. "I didn't like how he was talking to you, either. I could only do it because you were standing between us. I would have been in full-on panic mode, hugged around Magnus and unable to think of any way to help if you hadn't been here."

Those tiger eyes gleamed with some sort of secret light as he held her gaze. "I'll take that job, standing between you and the Rocky Garners of the world."

She sensed he meant something more than simply protecting her from the crude cop. But she was too long out of practice to believe her intuition when it came to a man's words. "What happens now? I'm assuming since you're a detective, you'll want to ask me some questions or do some investigating?"

Joel shook his head. "Not me. I called in reinforcements. They should be here any minute." He held up their hands between them and grinned as if he was surprised to see her still clinging to him. "I won't lie and say that KCPD isn't interested in nailing your ex for a myriad of crimes. Not that what happened here isn't upsetting, but, they'd like to pin something bigger than breaking and entering and threatening his ex-wife on him."

Mollie felt the warmth in her body drain out through the soles of her sneakers. "That makes logical sense. Augie has been indicted before without much success." She glanced at the threat on her door. "But you'll still make a report on this, right? I know in abuse and stalking cases, it's important to document, document, document. Show a pattern of behavior."

"I hate that you know that." His smile disappeared. "My friends will actually be the ones looking into this. I'm probably a little too close to the situation to be objective."

"Too close? What does that mean?"

"You and me?" He shrugged, clasping both hands around

hers now. "I'm feeling something here. Between us. It's new, and we're still getting to know each other better. I'm more likely to do whatever is best for you than whatever is necessary to solve the case and arrest whoever did this. So, I called an objective third party—my boss and his partner. Two veteran detectives. They'll get answers."

"Joel, this is too much. When I called, I just... I wanted some backup. A friendly face who knows a little about me and what I went through with Augie." She was shaking her head as she spoke. "I'm not comfortable being caught up in the middle of a big investigation. I don't know why he's coming after me like this now. I don't care if he gets married again. The terms of our divorce won't change."

"He doesn't pay you alimony?"

"God, no. I want nothing from that man. I just want him to leave me alone." Maybe she was shaking. Maybe she'd gone pale. Maybe she was obsessively fixated on the angry threats. *You know what I want. Make this right. Don't ruin this for me.*

It sounded like a reckoning was coming her way.

Keeping their hands linked together, Joel pulled her aside and hunched down to put his face in front of hers. "Hey. Look at me, not at that message on your front door. Mollie?"

When he said her name, she stopped fidgeting and met his gaze. She tilted her head to keep her focus on him as he straightened. "I didn't know who else to call. Maybe because we just had that long text conversation, but you were the first person I thought of."

"I'm glad. That's what friends do. You need me? I'm here." He rubbed his thumb across the back of her knuckles, and the warmth of that simple caress seeped beneath her skin and calmed her, allowing her to stay in the moment and think more rationally. "Maybe I'll need your help one day, and I'll call you to return the favor."

"What could I possibly do for you? I'm a waitress with post-traumatic stress. I'm perennially broke and scared of my own shadow."

"No, you're not. If you were weak, you wouldn't let me stand here holding your hand when I know physical contact can be a trigger for you. You wouldn't have stood up to Garner and stopped him from being a bully." A grin reappeared in the middle of his scruffy face. "You made him go away. I'll always be grateful for that."

She pooh-poohed his joke, and she almost laughed. "That's all I'm bringing to the table? My ability to make a phone call?" And then understanding dawned. "Oh. My connection to Augie." She tugged against Joel's grip. "That's why you want to be my friend. Because you think I can help you build a case against him."

He released her hand the moment she struggled but refused to back up. "Hey. Hear me out. Please. Maybe that's why I approached you initially. But that's not why I'm here today."

She eyed his hands as he held them out to either side without touching her. Even now he was respecting her need to be cautious about physical contact. That alone made her want him to touch her. But she petted the top of Magnus's head instead. "Why are you here?"

He scanned the hallways, perhaps making sure they were still alone before he continued. "You make me smile. You asked me to help your dog." He reached down to pet Magnus, too, and the tips of his fingers brushed against hers. "You just showed me you can think on your feet, even when you're upset. That's strength, Moll, and I admire that. You make me want to be the man I used to be. No, you make me want to be better than that guy."

She didn't pull away when he slid his hand over the top of hers.

"I can feel your hand growing cold under mine. You're holding yourself so still right now, I'm guessing you're trying to placate me and not draw any attention to yourself." His mouth hardened into a thin line. "You probably did that with your ex. A survival mechanism. And I hate that. I hate that you think I could be anything like him."

"I know you're not Augie." Those words were true. "But I still don't understand what you think you can get out of a relationship with me if it's not part of some plan to capture my ex-husband."

He slipped his fingers beneath her palm and pulled her hand away from the dog's head. She didn't resist when he gently chafed it between both of his to bring some circulation and warmth back to her fingers. "The short version of the story is… I think I need you."

"You think?"

He glanced up and down the hallways before turning his focus back to her. "I'm a man looking for a reason to get up in the morning. A man trying to make sense of the past few years of my life and where I go from here."

"And you're saying *I'm* that reason?"

"I don't know. But I know I've felt more excited about the last two days of my life than I did the last two years before that. It's because I got to see you and talk to you and get to know you. Knowing that you like me enough—trust me enough—to ask for my help with Magnus or when you're scared or overwhelmed, tells me that I need to be strong again." When Magnus heard his name, he raised his nose and nuzzled it against the clasp of their hands. Joel released one hand to pet the dog and praise him for being so attentive. "I need to care about something beyond the guilt and anger and resentment swirling around in my head 24/7."

"Guilt, anger, and resentment?" Mollie gave Magnus some attention, too, centering herself before asking, "Are you okay?"

"I'm working on it. But not like I should." Joel pulled her fingers from Magnus's fur and clasped them within his own again. When she didn't protest, he tightened his grip ever so slightly. "Talking to you makes me feel a little less broken, a little less useless."

"You're not useless."

"My last girlfriend betrayed me. She disappeared one night. I thought I was going to save her, but it was a trap. She was already dead from an overdose of opioids laced with fentanyl, and I got hurt because of her. I literally died and had to be resuscitated because of her."

"Died?" Her hand squeezed around his again. "Joel—"

"I'm not telling you this for sympathy. Just the opposite, in fact. It's nice to have someone who believes in me enough to call me when she's afraid and needs a favor. Not someone who's using me or setting me up to get hurt."

She uttered a breathless apology. "But I *am* using you."

Mollie felt the callused pad of his thumb gently stroking her hand again. Did he even realize he was doing it? Was it weird to feel this sensual pull to the man simply by holding hands? Maybe it was the way she felt cocooned between him and Magnus and the rest of the world. Maybe it was the fact that his touching her wasn't sending her into a panic. Maybe it was the fact that she hadn't been touched so caringly in a long time.

"Asking me for help is not using me." Joel's voice dropped to that gravelly timbre that sounded so masculine to her. "Telling a drug lord that I'm a cop working undercover in his organization in exchange for your next fix is."

Her mouth dropped open, aghast at the meaning behind the words he'd so casually shared. "She did that to you? The woman you loved?" Her gaze dropped to his muscular forearms, and she traced one of the puckers of scar tissue there with her fingertip. "Is that how you got hurt?"

When she looked up again, his jaw was tight and he simply nodded. She suspected there was a lot more to his story he wasn't sharing. "Cici didn't need me. She needed her next fix. My life, my heart, meant no more to her than a wad of cash. The dealer and his thugs she was working with explained that to me in very painful detail. I was the most convenient way to get her drugs."

Mollie needed a moment to process what he was telling her. Because of his limp and scars, and hardened personality, she thought he'd been in a traffic accident. But he'd been attacked, viciously, possibly by more than one person. More than the miracle of him surviving, he'd managed to get back to his normal life and become a cop again.

She'd finally stood up to Augie. She'd put together a plan, and finally made her escape. But she hadn't moved forward from her trauma the way Joel seemed to be trying to.

"Did the police capture them?" she asked quietly. "Were they arrested?"

He answered with a scary lack of emotion. "Cici's murder? The attempted murder of a cop? Any number of lesser crimes? They're in prison for the rest of their lives."

He'd found justice for the monstrous crimes committed against him. He'd survived, got justice, and was trying to move on. She wanted to do the same. She wanted the proof of Joel coming back from deception and violence and shattered hopes and dreams to inspire her to do the same. To do better than simply survive the way she had been. "Sounds like we're both searching for what's next or closure or something to make us feel a little less broken. Augie didn't need me, either. Lied to me all the time. He wanted a trophy wife who fit the standards of what he considered beautiful and accomplished to be a benefit to his career. To show his parents that he could find a good girl and settle down and take over the family business." The more she talked about what she'd been through, the easier it was to talk about it. "And the parts of me that didn't fit—my rural upbringing, a job he considered beneath him, sarcasm, brown hair—he changed or eliminated."

"He's an idiot for not embracing and protecting the treasure you are." *A treasure? Right.* She hadn't felt like anybody's treasure for a long time, and Joel's vehement defense made her a little uncomfortable. He must have sensed her retreating from him, and hastened to add, "Just continue to be real with me. Don't hold back your snark on my account. Don't lie about what you're dealing with or how you feel. Trust me to be there for you. To be enough to take care of whatever you need. I'll do my best to earn that trust. That's the only favor I ask."

"I'll try." She shook her head. "I don't know if I'm enough for anyone anymore—"

"That's your ex talking."

"—but *you* are." She reached down to pet Magnus, who seemed more relaxed now that she was alone with Joel. Smart dog. *She* was more relaxed with Joel here, too, even with the difficult conversation they'd just shared. Then, with that same hand, she reached up and rested it against Joel's chest. She felt his skin quiver beneath her touch, the warmth of finely sculpted muscle. She watched his nipples tighten into hard nubs and push against the cotton T-shirt he wore. The instinct to pull away from his body's natural reaction to being touched, to brace herself against the possibility of an unexpected blow blipped through her mind but quickly dissipated. This wasn't Augie. This was Joel. Her friend. He wasn't going to hurt her for reaching out. She could do something as normal as give him a reassuring pat on the chest, and she would be safe. "I will try to be the friend that you need, too. I promise. But I don't know how much help I can be with Augie. That's scary territory for me."

When she would have pulled away, Joel reached up and covered her hand with his, keeping it resting gently against him. "We'll figure it all out. Whether we stay friends or become something more? Who knows? Just give me a chance, okay?"

She considered what he was asking of her. And though they'd gotten off to a rocky start, she had to admit she wanted that same chance with him. "You didn't have to tell me about KCPD investigating Augie. You could have kept quiet and just used me to get what you needed."

"I'm not using you," he stated without equivocation. "The department isn't going to use you."

She heard a low-pitched conversation punctuated by a

laugh and nodded to the two men coming up the stairs behind Joel. "The decision may not be yours."

Mollie pulled away from Joel and reached for the comfort of Magnus instead. She recognized the short, wiry man
with the graying sideburns as Joel's friend from the diner.
But the man with him was as big as a house. His blond
hair receded slightly at the points of his forehead, but the
creases beside his eyes were laugh lines. She tried to focus
on those, and that he'd been laughing a moment ago, and
not on the fact that he towered over both the dark-haired
detective and Joel.

Joel turned to greet them. "Relax. I know these guys,
and they're the best detectives I've ever worked with." He
extended his arm to shake hands with both men.

"Boy, you don't get out much, do you, Standage," the big
man teased. "Better introduce us quick before your lady
friend decides big ol' me is one of the bad guys."

"I don't think that." She didn't sound very convincing
even to her own ears.

Joel reached back and snugged his hand around hers,
somehow finding her hand without even looking, as if a
magnet drew his hand to hers. As if he felt that same connection she'd imagined earlier, too. As if they hadn't just
shared a conversation that had knocked her sideways and
given her a whole lot to think about. "Don't give her any
grief, Josh. Rocky Garner was just here being his usual
pleasant self. This is Detective Josh Taylor, and his partner—my supervisor—Detective A. J. Rodriguez. This is
Mollie Crane."

"I apologize for anything Garner said." The big blond
man nodded a greeting before tucking his hands into the
pockets of his jeans and assuming a casual stance. "Please

know he's not representative of most of KCPD. Guys like him on the front line give the rest of us a bad name."

Mollie arched one eyebrow. "He's not doing you guys any favors."

Josh Taylor laughed. A. J. Rodriguez smiled. And Joel looked at her as if he was proud that she'd let her sarcasm peek out from her typically closed-off demeanor.

"I appreciate you two taking the lead on this," Joel said. "On the surface it looks like a typical B&E. But the picture, the threat, and the way it has been tossed inside makes me think the intruder was looking for something. Full disclosure? Mollie is August Di Salvo's ex-wife." Knowing it was necessary to share that information, she still shivered at being tied to the biggest mistake of her life. "With complications like that, I'm not ready to handle my own investigation."

"That's a crock—"

"I also have a certain prejudice against Di Salvo." Joel cut off his supervisor's protest. "If he is behind these terroristic incidents, as I suspect, then I want to make sure we build a case against him that can't be thrown out of court this time. I can provide any backup you need, but I feel better knowing you're running the show."

"Backup?" Josh smirked at A.J. "You going to set him straight, or should I?"

A.J. was clearly the more subdued partner. He nodded. "Josh, you see to Miss Crane, and I'll have a chat with our *amigo* here about resigning himself to being a paper pusher for the rest of his career."

Joel nodded toward Mollie. "This is too important for me to screw anything up."

A.J.'s face lost a bit of its cool demeanor. "You're gun-shy, Joel. Not incompetent. You need to find that badass cop I know you are again."

"This is gonna be an unpleasant conversation. Ma'am?" Josh gestured toward the apartment door with his big hand. "Have you had a chance to look around to see if anything was taken?"

She was hesitant to go with the larger man, even though he seemed polite and professional enough. "I didn't want to mess up the crime scene. I don't have much. The things I do value were with me."

"That's good." He thumbed over his shoulder to her apartment. "You want to just come hang out with me and skip the fireworks?" When Mollie didn't immediately respond, Josh Taylor nodded. "That's okay. I'll go scope things out and wait for a team from the crime lab to get here." With a nod from A.J., the blond detective took pictures of the newspaper and threats, as well as the splintered wood and scratches around the lock.

A.J. decided to postpone his lecture to Joel and turned his dark eyes on Mollie. "I'm not sure how long the crime lab will need to process the scene. Unfortunately, since the Di Salvo name is involved, this could be connected to other crimes we're looking at. You got a friend you can stay with tonight, ma'am?"

Other crimes. Oh, yeah. She knew Augie and some of his associates were involved in crimes far more serious than breaking and entering. But she wasn't ready to volunteer that kind of information. Her silence might be the only thing keeping her alive.

Although that threat on the door seemed to indicate that her time might be running out.

She pulled herself from the abyss of her thoughts and

heard Joel answering A.J.'s question for her. "She'll be staying with me. Once the scene is cleared tomorrow or the next day, I'll come back with her to salvage what we can and clean up the place."

Mollie tugged on Joel's hand. "Do I get a say in this?"

"Give me a minute, A.J.?" The older detective nodded. Joel pulled her aside. "Told you I was bossy. You weren't saying anything, and I thought maybe this was all getting to be too much. I should have asked and not decided for you. And after I just dumped all my emotional baggage on you, you may not want to spend any one-on-one time with me. *Do* you have a friend where I can drop you off tonight?"

"Corie's due date is tomorrow, so I'm not calling and imposing on her."

"Melissa?"

"They're at a family reunion with Sawyer's mom and brothers and their families this weekend. And Jessie Caldwell isn't really that kind of friend. Maybe more of a mentor, but I don't want to put her out. She's already helping me with Magnus." She didn't know if she was sad or embarrassed when she added, "I don't know who else I could impose upon."

"You're not an imposition. I have a fenced-in backyard. Plenty of room for Magnus to run off-leash. It's a safe neighborhood. My coffee maker works, and I've got beer in the fridge."

"Trying to sell me on your offer with beer and coffee?" Her gaze dropped to his waist and chest before meeting his eyes again. "I suppose you do have a gun and a badge."

He smiled at her subtle teasing. "There is that."

Mollie's hand found the top of Magnus's head, and she

drew in a calming breath, her decision made. "Do you have a spare bed?"

"Yes. Nothing fancy, but it's clean and comfortable."

"I come with a dog. I don't need fancy." She peeked around Joel's shoulder to A.J. "I'll be staying with Detective Standage tonight. You can call me there or on my cell phone if you need me."

"Sounds good." A.J. offered her an apologetic smile. "I really do need you to do a quick walk-through with Detective Taylor to see if you think anything is missing, or if there's another message besides what's on the door. Pack a bag if you need to. He'll let you know what things are safe to touch. I need to talk to Detective Standage for a few minutes." She nodded and headed for the door. "Sorry, but, the dog should probably remain out here. So, he doesn't accidentally disturb anything."

Her pulse leaped in a moment of panic. She didn't want to face anything Augie had left for her on her own. "But Magnus is my service dog."

Joel held his hand out for the leash. "I'll keep an eye on him—if you'll be okay without him for a few minutes. You've got this, Moll." She debated for a moment, then put her precious boy's leash in his hand and ordered the dog to stay. "We'll be at the door, so he can keep an eye on you."

Trust me to be there for you. To be enough to take care of whatever you need.

Baby steps, Mollie. She'd made huge strides in reclaiming some of her confidence and independence over the past two days. If she didn't want to be the prisoner of her fears the rest of her life, she needed to keep taking those steps forward. She could trust this man with her dog, at least. Right? "Okay."

Carefully finding her way around overturned chairs and food dumped from her cabinets and refrigerator, Mollie entered her apartment. She looked back to see Joel in a terse sotto voce conversation with his boss. About the crime scene? About her? About Augie?

Although the conversation was slightly heated, Joel sensed her looking, and turned to make eye contact with her. He winked before glancing down at Magnus. Her Belgian Malinois was lying down like a sphinx in the doorway, his tongue lolling out the side of his mouth as he panted, his dark eyes following her as she moved through the apartment after Detective Taylor.

Relaxed. Not concerned. Surrounded by people he seemed to trust.

Could she trust these men, too?

She was spending the night with a man. She hadn't done that since her divorce. And those first few weeks when she'd been staying at a homeless shelter, trying to save enough money for the down payment on this apartment, was the last time she'd had any kind of roommate besides Magnus.

She wasn't worried about staying with Joel. She didn't fear that he would try to hurt her, didn't worry that he had an ulterior motive for being kind to her and Magnus. She didn't dread the idea of sharing a meal with him and dropping her guard enough to be able to sleep.

Joel Standage was her friend. He'd answered her call for help twice today. And she got the feeling that he was just as leery of where this relationship might be going as she was. She was honest enough with herself to admit that there *was* a relationship developing here. And that was okay. With her. With Joel. And apparently, with Magnus.

Chapter Seven

The After Dark gentlemen's club wasn't in the best part of town. But the appointments of green leather, mahogany, and etched glass gave it the feeling of wealth and privilege. The place had been raided and closed down more than once in its checkered past, but under the new management of entrepreneur Roman Hess, After Dark had become less of a strip joint, and more of a place where wealth and discretion were the norm. The liquor was top-shelf, and the booths were appropriately secluded for meetings such as this one.

The host shooed away the server who had brought their drinks and welcomed the big man who slid into his seat on the far side of the table.

The big man downed his whiskey in one gulp, then wiped the back of his hand across his lips as he leaned back against the green leather with a self-satisfied sigh. "That went well."

"Is the cop you saw her with going to be a problem?"

"No. He's gimpy and washed up. I hear he's been stuck behind a desk for the past few months. He got lucky with the car yesterday. If you'd wanted me to actually hit them, I could have." He smirked a laugh. "Should have clipped the dog, though. I'm not a big fan of that mutt."

Although the host wanted to be there to witness first-hand how Mollie Di Salvo got knocked off her high horse each and every step of the way, there was the practical matter of distancing oneself from the crimes to maintain plausible deniability. That's what willing employees like this one were for. "How did she look when you saw her today?"

"Scared out of her mind."

"Serves her right. I haven't had a moment's peace since she dared to defy the Di Salvo name."

The big man rested his forearms on the table and fisted one hand within the other. "I didn't find what you're looking for."

No apology was necessary. "I didn't think you would. That country bimbo is smarter than she looks. I imagine she has more than one copy and a couple of contingency plans to keep them hidden."

A smug smile spread across the big man's expression. "I did put my hands on everything she owns in that ratty little apartment—from dumping out the dog food to slicing up her boring cotton panties."

"She really has fallen a long way from the life she once had with us."

"I'll bet she misses everything she gave up."

"Threw away, you mean." It was hard to compare the beautiful, polished blonde who'd lived at the mansion for two years with the ragamuffin brunette who waited tables at a diner—poorly, too, if reports were accurate. "I've worked too hard to get where I am. I'm not about to let her get her grubby waitress hands on any of it. And I won't allow her to ruin what the Di Salvo family has built."

The big man nodded his agreement. "What's the next step?"

"We keep her off-balance, punish her for her disobedience. When the time is right and I do get my hands on her, I want her to fall apart and beg to give me everything I want."

"Right before we kill her?"

The host gave a firm no. "I'm not getting my hands dirty. That's what I'm paying you for."

"I appreciate you giving me this opportunity. Done wonders for my bank account. I'll be waiting for my next assignment."

"Soon. I'll let you know." An envelope thick with cash exchanged hands. "I reward loyalty like yours. Mollie Di Salvo doesn't know the meaning of loyalty. That was her mistake. Keep up the good work."

The big man tucked the envelope inside the front of his jacket, understanding that he was being dismissed. "What about her dog?"

"Expendable."

"And the cop?"

"Also expendable." The host held up a hand for the server to return with another drink. "All that matters is getting what's mine. And making her pay for causing me so much trouble."

MOLLIE STOOD ON the front porch of Joel's gray bungalow as she hugged her arms around herself and watched the rain fall from the night sky. Lightning flashed, momentarily lighting up the clouds above her, and the drumbeat of thunder rumbled in the distance. The hairs on her arms pricked to attention with the electricity in the air.

Some people might find the storm unsettling or even frightening, she supposed. But she loved being out in nature like this. After the intense heat of the past few days, a thunderstorm had been inevitable. She loved the normalcy of it all. Hot, moist air rose into cooler air higher in the atmosphere. The moving air charged the atmosphere. Water vapor formed as the air cooled, lightning flashed, and rain fell from the sky. The process repeated itself over and over. Everything felt right in Mother Nature's world tonight.

She missed nights out in the trees and hills of the Ozarks, where she could smell the rain and feel cocooned from the rest of the world by a summer storm. Her vandalized apartment had no balcony, and the metal fire escape outside her window wasn't where she wanted to stand when there was lightning. And outdoor activities beyond a stuffy garden party were generally frowned upon at the Di Salvo estate. Joel's home might still be within the city limits of Kansas City, but the old neighborhood with the charming small houses and well-tended yards felt a lot closer to the country than where she lived in the City Market area north of downtown.

She breathed in the ozone-scented air, closed her eyes, and savored the damp mist from the rain splashing her cheeks and frizzing her hair.

"I'd feel better if you two came inside." Joel's gravelly voice matched the rumbles of thunder and darkness of the night.

She smiled at the unexpected sense of familiarity and security she felt here. She spread her fingers across the limestone rocks that still held some of the heat from the day. "I love your front porch. These rock pillars make me think of Granny's house. We used to sit out on her porch when it rained. It was always so cool and refreshing. No central air."

"It's not the storm I'm worried about."

"Oh." She turned to see him waiting in the shadows behind the screen door. He was leaning heavily on a metal cane tonight. She wondered if the same barometric pressure changes she'd been enjoying made his injuries ache more than usual. "Do you really think Augie's men are out in this?" She pointed to the porch lamp beside him. "I left the light off."

"Good call." He pushed the door open wider and gestured for her to come in. "But my gun and badge still think inside and out of sight is a safer place for you to be until we can figure out what your ex is up to. Come on, boy." Magnus immediately rolled to his feet and trotted indoors to find a drier, softer place to snooze, no doubt. Mollie hesitated at the threshold, saddened to be reminded that every decision in her life seemed to go back to her ex-husband and his impact on her life. "Unless you're afraid to be alone in the house with me."

"That's not it." Mollie tilted her gaze to Joel's, marveling at how his beautiful eyes gleamed in the lamplight from inside his living room. She couldn't help but notice, too, that while she was dressed in sweatpants and a long-sleeved shirt in deference to the weather and the air-conditioning in his house, Joel wore a pair of gym shorts and a faded gray KCPD T-shirt that clung to his biceps and gave her a glimpse of more of the tattoo swirling around his left arm. Her pulse beat at a faster tempo as she imagined pushing his sleeve out of the way and tracing her fingers completely around the intricate markings.

Good grief. She'd never been obsessed with any man's body the way she was with Joel's. Not even Augie's back when she'd been happy with him. When she realized her nostrils were flaring as she breathed in the clean, spicy scent of his skin and damp hair after his shower, she turned away and hurried through the front door.

She sat on the tweedy black and tan plaid couch where she'd been reading a book while he showered and changed after dinner. The throw blanket he'd offered her earlier was piled on the oak floor beside her feet, and Magnus was stretched across it with his head resting on his teddy bear. With Magnus's dog bed out of commission, Joel had been kind enough to give the dog permission to make himself at home with his things, although she'd drawn the line at letting the dog up on the couch. Dog hair and drool weren't the easiest things to clean up.

Mollie heard the screen door latch and two locks engage on the interior door before Joel spoke again. "Then what is it? Do you need something? I'd rather not run to the store in this weather, but I will. I can loan you a sweatshirt if you're cold. Or, I've got a spare toothbrush from my last trip to the dentist if you forgot yours."

Wincing in sympathy, she watched pain jar through his clenched teeth as he limped around the black leather ottoman that served as a coffee table and practically fell into his seat at the far corner of the sofa. He leaned the metal cane against the armrest and immediately dug his fist into the scars of his thigh above his right knee. "How much pain are you in?" she asked.

"Answer my question first. Are you okay being in here with me tonight?"

"Joel," she protested.

"Moll," he mimicked right back.

She would have laughed at his teasing delivery if she wasn't worried about him. "On a scale of one to ten, what's your pain level right now?"

"You're not my nurse."

"No. But I do have some experience dealing with healing fractures and sore muscles."

Joel nailed her with a look that conveyed a depth of anger he thankfully held in check. "I'm never going to let that man touch you again."

Yeah, yeah. Augie was a monster who'd screwed up her life and left her a fragile shell of her former self. But one thing she *could* still do well was focus on someone else, especially if that someone was in pain, and she could help. "One to ten?"

The grin that softened the angles of his face made her think she'd imagined the anger from a moment before. "You were a handful for your granny growing up, weren't you. Sarcastic. Stubborn. Strong. That's the real you, isn't it."

She faced him on the couch, settling her back against the armrest and curling her legs beneath her. She plucked at an imaginary piece of lint on the butt-hugging sweats she wore and nonchalantly responded. "I can neither confirm nor deny any worrisome late nights I might have caused Granny."

He laughed out loud.

THAT WAS THE moment when Joel realized he was in deep trouble with this woman.

At first glance, Mollie Crane was fragile and scattered and in need of a rescuer—just like Cici Martin had been. And yeah, she triggered his need to help and protect her, to be needed by someone. But unlike Cici, who'd lost her way to drugs and a quick fix for her pain, Mollie had courage and a sense of humor and was fighting for her own salvation every step of the way. She turned to a dog, not drugs, to cope. She worked hard at a job she might not love, found herself a decent place to live, bought herself a rattletrap of a car he fully intended to check out before he let her drive another centimeter in it, and made her own way in the world. She'd escaped her violent prison, and still had the strength to make a joke and care about others. He'd seen her interact with the people she worked with at the diner. It felt as if she might even care a little bit about him.

"That's the Mollie I like. Do you mind if I put my feet up?" She didn't protest when he turned sideways and stretched his legs across the couch. It was a big piece of furniture, and with her curled up like that, his toes barely touched the edge of the cushion where she sat. "Storms like this and changes in the weather wreak havoc on my rebuilt knees. Plus, I lost my favorite cane in your alley yesterday, so I've been walking and running without it too much today. I'm probably at a four or five. The hot shower helped. I'll take a couple of ibuprofens when I go to bed. Mostly, I just need to get off them for a while."

"Do you have enough room to stretch out?" she asked.

"Yes. Now, answer my question." He was really hoping for an answer that wouldn't make him feel guilty for issuing the invitation earlier that evening. "Are you okay here? Or is being with me stressing you out?"

"I'm fine."

He suspected as much after she'd put her foot down about his pain and teased him with a silly answer about her childhood, but he still breathed a sigh of relief to hear her say the actual words. "I'm glad."

"I certainly don't want to be in my apartment with a busted lock tonight. Even with Magnus, I wouldn't feel safe. I'm sure I wouldn't sleep." She shrugged. "I don't know if it's the house or the storm isolating us from the threat that's out there, or you, but I feel safe. I enjoy our conversations. I know there are some heavy issues we have to discuss regarding Augie. But I appreciate that you're not pushing me. To be honest, I haven't felt this…normal…with a man in a long time."

"Normal?" Was that akin to *comfortable*?

"It's hard to explain." She tucked a dark curl behind her ear and caught her bottom lip between her teeth in a soft smile that zinged straight to his groin. He wanted to taste that bottom lip for himself, soothe the spot where she nipped it with the stroke of his tongue. But she continued to talk, and he wasn't going to do a damned thing to scare her away from the easy conversations they'd been sharing all evening. So, he continued to rub at the knotted muscles in his thigh and pretend that this was how every evening between them might go. "The storm reminds me of where I grew up. I love your house. It's small, but it feels like a home. It's easy, relaxed here. I don't feel I have to dress for company or choose the right fork to eat with."

"We had pizza and beer and used our fingers," he reminded her. "I'm not that fancy."

She patted her tummy, indicating that she was still full from the takeout meal they'd picked up on the way here. "My ex-mother-in-law would have had a coronary if she caught anyone eating on the couch watching the ball game like we did tonight. And pizza was food for the hired help, not the Di Salvos. If Bernadette caught me eating anything but a canapé or hors d'oeuvres with my fingers, she would have told Edward. Edward would have told Augie. Then there'd be a conversation about me forgetting my station and embarrassing him."

"Did your in-laws live with you?" She was talking about her past. This was the information he needed. He knew he should keep her sharing intel about her previous life, but hell if he wanted to talk about anything except the two of them.

"The Di Salvo estate where you worked for a few months belongs to Augie's parents. *We* lived with *them*. Separate wings of the mansion, but still…" She sighed heavily. "Unless they were traveling, or he was on a business trip, Edward and Bernadette were there."

"Nothing says *honeymoon* like having your in-laws on the premises."

But his joke didn't elicit a smile. "Edward and Augie had offices in the city. But they conducted a lot of their business at the house. Dinner parties were contract negotiations. Business associates would stay in a guest room and use the home office for strategy meetings. Late-night drinks were for problem solving."

"What kind of problems?"

"Augie could be a loose cannon." Obviously. "He'd alienate clients with a temper tantrum or sleep with someone's wife. I learned too late that marrying me was supposed to clean up his reputation." She pumped her fist as if she was repeating a familiar cheer. "Sweet, all-American girl. No family to speak of, but a straight-A student who hadn't gotten herself knocked-up before graduation or caused any scandals. Pretty enough to be arm candy, but not ambitious enough to be a threat to the family." She shook her head, no doubt recalling what a sham her marriage had become by the time he'd met her. "I was in a vulnerable place when I met him. Granny had just died. I thought I was gaining a devoted husband and a loyal family who cared about me.

But I was just window dressing. Once I got to know the real family, I became a prisoner, a puppet to play whatever part they needed from me."

"I'm so sorry. You deserve so much better."

She nodded. "Because I was so unhappy, *I* became the problem sometimes."

"You?" Since she'd been isolated from him during most of his assignment there, he hadn't realized just how much of the family business pertained to her. She could be a gold mine of information for KCPD. But the more he got to know her, the less he liked the idea of looking to her for a lead on their investigation. "What possible problem could they blame on you?"

She plucked at that invisible piece of lint again. "Volunteering for the wrong charity. I'm trained to teach. I wanted to volunteer with schoolchildren, but that didn't have the client base the Di Salvos were looking for. I needed to schmooze with wealthier people. Set them up for meetings with Augie."

"I'll bet you're a good teacher. Do you miss it?"

She gave him half a smile. "I keep my hand in it by tutoring Corie's son, Evan, and Jessie Caldwell's foster kids."

"Why are you waiting tables? Isn't there a demand for good teachers?"

Her gaze dropped to the dog snoring at the foot of the sofa, and he knew he'd hit a sensitive spot for her. But before he could turn the conversation to something less upsetting for her, she answered. "Edward is friends with one of the school board members. He got a note slipped into my personnel file that says I'm a danger to children. That I'm mentally unstable."

"No way." Joel fisted his hand on the back of the sofa

and scooted closer to her. "You have panic attacks brought about by a traumatic marriage that they're responsible for. People with disabilities work in schools all the time, and yours is minor compared to some of the stuff I've heard about. They're all good people. Good teachers. Just because they're in a wheelchair or blind or need a service dog doesn't make them a threat to anybody."

She gaped at him through his entire defense of her. Too late, he realized he was probably scaring the crap out of her.

"I'm sorry," he quickly apologized. He opened his fist and pulled it back into his lap. "What you said pissed me off. I didn't mean to yell at you."

"You weren't yelling at me. You were angry on my behalf. I can tell the difference." She didn't leave the room. She didn't reach for her dog. She didn't even flinch away from his toes pressed against her knee. His brave, backbone-of-steel girl simply nodded and quietly answered. "That's the kind of power they have. If they want something, they know someone or pay someone to make it happen. Or they pay someone to make it go away."

"Like you?"

She was silent for so long, Joel thought he'd pushed too hard, got too emotional, and the conversation was over. But her words surprised him. "I left on my own terms. I didn't take a penny from them." Her fingers rubbed against the outline of the locket she wore beneath her long-sleeved T-shirt. "The break-in at my apartment? I'm sure they were looking for something I took from Augie." She reached down to pet Magnus now, as the conversation became more stressful for her. "I had to blackmail him to get him to sign the divorce papers and then leave me alone. He threatened to kill me if I ever left him. And I believed him. I had to do something to get the advantage over him."

Blackmail? Forget the fact that technically Mollie had committed a crime if what she was saying was true. This could be the mother lode of information A.J. thought she could give them. "What could you possibly take that would inspire the kind of violence you've seen the past couple of days?"

"Evidence of illegal activities. Money laundering. Pay-offs. Intimidation tactics."

Bingo.

But there was a catch. She nibbled on her bottom lip again, and it was all Joel could do not to slide across the sofa and take her in his arms and tell her she never had to talk about any of this again. "I know that's what you want from me. That's what A.J. and Josh want from me. But I can't give that to you. The moment I hand over the information I have, I lose any leverage I have over Augie and his family. They'll come after me. They'll silence me. The only advantage I have is that they don't know where I've hidden the information, or how many copies I've made, or who I've arranged for it to be distributed to should anything happen to me. I'm sorry, Joel, but I can't do it."

Magnus sat up and laid his head in her lap, no doubt sensing the same fear he felt radiating off her in waves.

"You have evidence that can implicate the Di Salvos?" Joel felt compelled to point out the same facts A.J. and Josh would. "Withholding evidence is a crime."

She continuously stroked Magnus's head, but her pretty blue eyes were focused squarely on him. "So is blackmail. If it helps any, I never took any money from them. Just the divorce and my freedom. Arrest me if you have to, but keeping the evidence hidden is how I'm staying alive."

And that's where the facts he needed for this investigation ended.

After a few moments, Mollie gave Magnus permission to lie down again. "Good boy. You go night-night with Teddy, okay?" Joel imagined the dog was giving him the stink eye for upsetting his mama before the Malinois stretched out again on the floor in front of the couch.

That was probably his cue to shut up and get to bed himself before he said or did anything else that would scare Mollie away from the tentative trust they shared. "I'll recheck the windows and doors, make sure everything is secure before we turn in."

"You're not going to ask me any more questions about Augie?"

She was frowning when he met her gaze. She didn't yet understand that her well-being was more important to him than any investigation. "No."

Joel started to pull away. But Mollie grabbed his ankles and stopped him. "The round, puckered scars on your knees. Are those bullet wounds?"

He tugged against her grasp. "You don't want to hear my story tonight."

Her grip tightened almost painfully, and he suddenly had the insight that maybe she needed to talk about something else besides August Di Salvo so she could fall asleep and not have nightmares. Or simply fall asleep at all. Once she realized she was still holding his legs, she eased her clutch on him and stroked her fingers along the sides of his calves. Her fingertips felt like heaven against his skin. But she suddenly pulled them away. "Is it okay if I touch you?"

He nodded. "You don't have to ask. You can touch me anytime you want."

"But you're so respectful of my needs. You always ask, or make sure I know it's you."

"Those are your boundaries, and I'll respect them as long as you need me to. Mine are different. Not everybody gets permission, but you do." He held out his hand until she rested her fingers against his palm. "Yes. I've been shot in both legs."

Her grip tightened around his for a moment before she pulled away to settle her hands back against his legs. "You've had surgery to replace both knees?"

"Yes."

"You sound so cold and clinical when you talk about your injuries."

"My therapist says that, too." Her eyes opened wide at the news he'd been seeing the KCPD psychologist. Well, that he was supposed to be reporting for more sessions with her. "But that's how I cope. I keep my emotions pinned down, so they don't get in the way of doing my job."

She arched a skeptical eyebrow. "Your job pushing papers?"

He poked her knee with his big toe. "Smart-ass."

Thankfully, she let the topic drop and resumed her curiosity and concern about his pain.

"I always found that alternating a hot washcloth and cold compresses helped when my injuries were healing." She climbed up onto her knees and scooted between his feet, forcing his legs apart. "Once the bruising had faded, a good massage stimulated the blood flow and helped the aches feel better." She leaned forward and wrapped her hands around the thigh he'd been rubbing himself. When she dug her thumbs into the ligaments and muscle above his knee, he winced. But it was a good kind of pain. The initial rebellion of his knotted muscles calmed a bit with each pass of her fingers across his skin. "Wow. You're tight as a crossbow. You've been overcompensating for your painful joints. No wonder you're limping."

"Crossbow?" he bit out through his tightly clenched jaw. Her strong hands and nimble fingers created a friction that warmed his skin and settled into his muscles. The massage hurt at first, but he exhaled sharply when the cramp unknotted itself and the pain finally eased to an ache rather than the stabbing sensation that had practically crippled him.

She inclined her head to the book on the ottoman. "You had a copy of the first Bonecrusher Chronicles on your bookshelf. I love that series."

He nodded. He liked that they were both fans of the high fantasy series. "Larkin Bonecrusher carries a crossbow."

She smiled in a pretty apology as she continued to work the kinks out of his leg muscles. "Don't take this the wrong way, but you don't look like a reader. Yet you've got a ton of books over there."

Genuinely curious now, he asked, "What does a reader look like?"

"You know. Skinny. Glasses. Socially awkward." She slapped a hand over her mouth and blushed. "I am so sorry. That was a terrible stereotype." She went back to the massage, focusing intently on her work and refusing to meet his gaze. "Readers come in all shapes and sizes and personalities, of course. I just meant that you seem more like a man of action, that you prefer to be outdoors rather than curled up on the couch reading like I was." He grinned when she waved her hand at him, indicating his face and body, without looking at him. "With all your badness and spiky hair and scars and scruffy face and all."

His badness? Joel chuckled and extended a hand toward her. "May I?"

She nodded when she understood his intent. "You don't have to ask every time you want to touch me, either. As long as I know it's you."

"Thank you." He reached out with one finger to tap her chin and tilt her gaze up to his. "I'm an old pro. I had a lot of time to read during my recovery. Besides, that's how I got my brothers to sleep every night. I'd read stories to them. It's still how I get myself to sleep most nights."

"I like that. I read, too, to escape reality long enough to calm my thoughts and relax."

He pulled back and leaned against the arm of the sofa, savoring her willingness to touch him and truly appreciating the massage. "I don't know what kind of badass you think I am. Blending in and looking like every other guy on the street is my stock-in-trade. Yeah, I work out and take care of myself. But I've always had a forgettable face. Brown hair, brown eyes. I'm easy to overlook. Makes me a perfect candidate for undercover work."

Her hands stilled above his knees. "That's not true."

"No, I was pretty good at UC work. Right up until my last case."

"What I meant was that there's nothing about you that's forgettable. Your eyes are more golden than brown. That first night I met you, I thought of a tiger. And tonight, they're reflecting the light the way a cat's would. Your voice is sexy—low and gravelly, like you just woke up or you just had…"

Her eyes got wide, and she blushed. *Sex.* She was thinking about him and sex together in the same sentence.

Joel adjusted his position on the couch to hide his body's reaction to her innocently provocative words. He was in more trouble than he thought. He wasn't just attracted to Mollie's sass and vulnerability. He was falling hard and fast for a woman who'd been so damaged by her previous relationship that she might never be able to love again.

She curled her fingers into her fists and pulled away to hug her arms around herself. Just as quickly, she was gesturing to him again. "You're funny one minute and over-the-top manly the next. You've got muscles and tats. Not everyone is into those, but they give you that bad boy vibe—unless those words on your arm are a Shakespearean sonnet."

"They're not. If you want to read my ink, all you have to do is ask. I just didn't think you were the kind of woman who would be into tattoos."

Her eloquent hands landed on her hips, and she gave him a confused look. "What kind of woman do you think I am?"

"Very high-class. Out of place in a working-class neighborhood like the City Market or Brookside. A lady through and through. Way out of my league."

"And you claim I misread *you*?" Any trace of embarrassment was gone. Now she was just huffy, and it was cute as hell. "Joel Standage, I was raised in the country by my granny. Not my grandmother or my grand-mama. We lived in a little town in the Ozarks. I went from kindergarten through twelfth grade, all in the same building. I can make biscuits and gravy from scratch that would make your daddy weep. I can change my own tire on a car and fix a toilet. I played second base on my high school softball team, and we made it to State my senior year and I had the best double-play completion stats in the entire state that year. I had a twang in my voice until I met Augie in college, and he convinced me I could go further in life without it. But it sneaks back in now that I don't have to watch every word I say. I try to be a lady, but I'm not some prissy girlie-girl with a stick up her butt like you're describing."

Food. Cars. Softball. Snark. He was so hot for her right now.

He realized his mouth was hanging open, and he snapped it shut. "You can make biscuits and gravy?"

She puffed out a breath that stirred the wavy bangs on her forehead. "That's what you got out of my impassioned speech?"

"I love biscuits and gravy."

She smiled and shook her head. "You come off as a streetwise bad boy, most of the time. But you're just a little boy inside."

"A little boy who likes biscuits and gravy," he mock pouted. She laughed out loud, and Joel smiled, thinking she didn't do that nearly often enough. "And if I'm around, you won't be changing your own tire or fixing the damn toilet. You don't have to change who you are to meet some society standard that the Di Salvos want you to be. That's not what makes you a lady."

She uncurled her legs from beneath her and scooted back to the far end of the couch, pausing as she considered his words. He could see the expression on her face change when she made a decision.

Leaning toward him, she rested her hand lightly over his shinbone. "Do you want me to fix you breakfast in the morning?"

"Yes. If you can find something more than a box of cereal in my pantry, I would love to eat anything homemade."

"You don't cook?"

"I fix cars."

"Huh? I don't get the connection."

"I never learned how to cook. Mom left us, remember? I learned how to fix cars. I'm good with engines, not ovens."

"How did you feed your brothers when you were taking care of them?"

"I can grill burgers or hot dogs outside, and whip up a mean box of mac and cheese. And I can zap anything in the microwave. But I don't have the kind of skills you're talking about."

He was suddenly, vibrantly aware of her hand on his leg. "I'm sure you have other useful skills, Detective."

Well, hell's bells. Was that sexual innuendo from Mollie Crane? Or did he just want it to be? The part of him swelling inside his shorts voted yes. Joel swung his feet to the floor, grabbed his cane, and stood before he embarrassed her with his physical reaction to her. "It's late. You must be getting tired. Does Magnus need to go out one more time? When do you need to get up for work? You can use the alarm on your phone, or I've got an old clock in my dresser."

Mollie stepped over Magnus and hurried to block his path on the other side of the ottoman. "Did I say something wrong? You act like you're trying to make a quick getaway."

When this whole assignment started, he promised himself not to lie to her. He wasn't going to start lying now. Feeling like the luckiest man in the world to know she'd given him permission to touch her, he reached out to capture a tendril of rich brown hair that had fallen over her cheek. He watched the tendril curl around his finger before he brushed it back and tucked it behind her ear. Then he sifted his fingertips into the silky weight of her hair at her nape and cupped the side of her neck and jaw. "I like you, Mollie Crane. More than a guy you need as a friend should. Some of tonight feels like flirting, like we're on a date and really getting to know each other because it's leading to something... I'm trying to be a good guy and walk away while I still can."

"A date? Can you imagine how out of practice I am at picking up signals and flirting after being married to Augie? And you have no idea how good it feels to have somebody touch me, and be able to touch him, and not freak out." Instead of pulling away, she turned her cheek into his palm. Her skin was warm and soft against his. "I'm sorry if I made things awkward or you thought I was leading you on."

"I don't. You have nothing to apologize for."

She smiled at being let off the hook so easily. "I've been scared for so long, it felt good to relax with you tonight and be comfortable enough with you to resurrect a little of who I used to be. I mean, I do have brains and a personality. I have history besides being a Di Salvo. I care about people. I haven't always lived from one panic attack to the next."

He picked up on the same word he'd been feeling since the moment they'd reconnected at the dog park. "You're *comfortable* with me?"

"Yes. I'm surprised at how quickly I'm learning to trust you. It's like I've known you for a lot longer than a couple of days and a couple of random meetings in the past."

"It's like fate kept trying to push us together, but we weren't in the right place in our lives to do anything about it until now."

Nodding her agreement with his fanciful notion, she wound her fingers around his wrist, holding his hand against her face, linking them together. "Full disclosure? I think I also have the hots for you, and I'm wondering if I can ever be *normal* with a man again. If I can build the kind of trust necessary to be intimate with someone."

Joel burned with the implication of what she was saying. "Did Di Salvo…?"

"Yes. He forced me. Whether or not I was in the mood didn't matter if Augie wanted sex. Thankfully, he always had a girlfriend or two on the side, so it didn't happen too often."

Not too often? That didn't make it any easier to hear how that bastard had brutalized her. "I'm going to kill that son of a bitch."

She shifted her hand to cup his unshaven jaw, mirroring the hold he had on her. "No. You're not. If I'm lucky, you're going to be very patient with me, and you're going to conduct a thorough police investigation. And then we're going to put him away in prison, where somebody else can kill him for us."

Joel's eyebrows rose at the quick addendum. She'd not only calmed his need for retribution, but she'd said *we* and *us*, letting him know that she was feeling the bond growing between them, too. "Yes. To all that. I shouldn't like your vindictive streak, but I do."

She glanced down at the tent in his gym shorts and pulled away without putting any distance between them. "Thank you for being stronger than I am tonight. Maybe one day you won't feel you have to hide that from me, and we can make out on your couch. Hopefully, I won't freak out on you and be a disappointment."

"No way could you disappoint me. We're *comfortable* with each other, remember? That's our motto now. Making out with you will blow my mind, I'm sure. Anything beyond that will be a true gift. And if it never happens, that's okay, too. We'll go as hot and heavy or slow and careful as we need to, and I will treasure every moment."

He was surprised when she grasped his forearm and turned it so she could read the words inked there. "Are you sure this isn't a sonnet on your arm? You spout some pretty sweet poetry when you want to."

"Nah." He pulled up his sleeve so she could read the full message. "It's part of the Armed Forces prayer. I got it in honor of my father and brothers."

She read the words out loud. "'Teach us not to mourn those who have died in the service of the Corps, but rather to gain strength from the fact that such heroes have lived.'" Tears glistened in her eyes when she tilted her gaze back to his. "Oh, Joel. This applies to you, too. It's beautiful. Your family must be so proud." She stunned him when she leaned in and kissed the words above his elbow. Then she lifted her gaze to his. Keeping her hand braced against his bicep, she stretched up to gently kiss his stubbled jaw, his cheek, and finally the corner of his mouth.

He couldn't have held back the groan of desire that rumbled in his throat if his life depended on it. Mollie was kissing him. Battered by life, but never broken, she sweetly, boldly slid her lips against his. She'd put her hands on him and stirred his body to life. But her soft, sweet lips were stoking a fire deeper inside.

Joel dropped his cane to the rug and cupped her face with both hands, tunneling his fingers into the silky weight of her hair. He kissed her chastely at first, pressing his closed mouth against hers, not wanting to frighten her just as much as he *did* want to claim everything she offered him. She didn't protest when he angled her head from one position to another, seeking the perfect link between their lips. And each new taste was as perfect as the last.

He felt each fingertip digging into the muscles of his arm, and her open palm skimming along the textures of his scratchy stubble and the short, damp hair at the back of his head. When her lips parted to capture his bottom lip between her own, Joel felt his temperature spike. In response, he stroked his tongue along the plump arc of her lower lip and the sculpted arch of her pliant upper lip, asking for permission to enter. Her warm gasp across his skin was more of a turn-on than the most seductive words. Her lips parted and her tongue tentatively reached out to touch his. Their tongues danced around each other for a few seconds before he slipped inside her mouth and claimed the generous gift of her willing mouth.

He tasted a slight tang of beer on her tongue, or maybe that was his own. He breathed in the delicate flowery scent of whatever lotion or soap she'd used on her face. Their bodies never touched. It was hands in hair and lips and tongues, exploring and claiming, giving and demanding, and absolute heaven.

This woman was brave yet fragile. She was strong but delicate. She was generous yet cautious. She was more than everything he wanted in a woman. With this kiss? This moment? He knew that she was everything he needed.

With a nervous chuckle in her throat, Mollie broke off the kiss. He felt the gusts of her uneven breaths against his neck and knew he was breathing just as erratically. But he didn't try to re-engage her. He didn't pull her into his body the way he longed to. He didn't tug on her hair to tip her head back so he could kiss his fill of her. Any physical contact between them needed to be on her terms.

Mollie tilted her dark blue eyes up to his. "Sorry. I liked that. I loved it. I've never kissed a man with beard stubble before. It's…sexy…like a hundred extra little caresses against my skin." Her hands had settled on his shoulders, and her gaze dropped to his lips. "You're a really good kisser. Or, maybe I've never been kissed right before… You probably wanted something more, but I'm feeling a little overwhelmed…"

"Hey." He pressed his thumb against her slightly swollen lips to silence her rambling and keep her nerves from spiraling out of control. "Treasure. Every. Moment." He whispered the heartfelt promise before planting a silly kiss on the tip of her nose and another to her forehead, where he lingered long enough to inhale the fragrance of her skin and hair once more. "I don't think I've ever been kissed that right before, either. Thank you."

He bent down to pick up his cane. His gaze swept past her taut nipples poking against the thin cotton of her shirt and he smiled. It was nice to know he wasn't the only one whose clothes felt a little confining right now.

Mollie stepped back and called Magnus to her side. "Magnus is fine for tonight. I'll use my own alarm. Good night, Joel."

He reached out and tucked her short hair behind her ear, tracing his fingertips around her delicate earlobe before pulling away. Knowing he could touch her like this soothed him, even as the possibility of getting closer to her excited him. "Good night, Moll."

She gifted him with a smile before turning away and

ordering Magnus to heel. Joel watched her walk down the hallway to the guest bedroom. He was still leaning on his cane and watching as her door snicked shut behind her.

What the hell was he doing here? He wasn't the best man for Mollie's protection detail. He probably wasn't even the best man to be her friend. She needed someone who wasn't as broken as he was. She needed better.

But after tonight, after getting close to her, he wasn't giving the job to anybody else.

So, he was damn well going to figure out how to be a better man for her.

Protector, friend, dog walker, lover—whatever she needed, he wanted to be able to give that to her.

And that meant getting rid of his cane, getting out from behind a desk, and getting back to being the cop—and the man—he'd been before his world had imploded.

Chapter Eight

Joel holstered his weapon, counted down from three, then pulled out his Glock and fired the last three bullets in rapid succession into the outline of a man on the downrange target.

Then he dropped the magazine from the butt of the gun and opened the firing chamber to make sure both were empty before setting them on the shelf in front of him. He was aware of the dark-haired man waiting patiently behind him in the booth at the firing range in the basement of the Fourth Precinct building. But he wanted to complete this round of training to make sure he was good enough to be responsible for Mollie's safety. He was trying to find his way back to being good enough for her, period.

He'd known when A. J. Rodriguez had slipped into the back of the booth a few minutes earlier, but he was focused on the task at hand. He appreciated his boss's inimitable patience and knew that was half the reason A.J. had earned his legendary reputation at KCPD. Joel removed his safety goggles and earphones and pushed the button to bring the target forward.

A.J. pulled off his earphones and hung them on the hook beside Joel's safety gear. "Working off some steam? Or getting your skills in shape so you can go back to your real job?"

"I'm trying to come back from being an idiot and dying. I *need* to come back."

Joel studied the paper target hanging in front of him. Most of his shots hit center mass. But there were three wide shots that would only wing a perp he was trying to bring down or annoy him with the boo-boo on his arm.

A.J. stepped up beside him to check the results, too. "Looks like your aim is drifting a shade to the right. You still favoring that leg?"

Joel felt almost normal right now, but he hadn't gone for his morning run or taken the stairs to the third floor more than once today. He was still relishing the fabulous, unexpected massage he'd gotten from Mollie last night. Although he hated knowing how she'd become such an expert in pressure points, pinched nerves, and massages, she could do some amazing things with those hands. "It's doing better. I don't think it's a hundred percent yet. I don't always need the cane. I just have to be careful about wearing myself out."

"You'll get there."

"Or I'll learn to compensate."

A.J. waited while Joel reassembled and reloaded his gun and secured it in his holster. "I got your message you wanted to meet. Is this about Miss Crane, or you?"

"Both."

"Walk me to my office?" A.J. pushed open the door and gave a salute to the officer on watch while Joel checked out of the range. "We can talk on the elevator ride up."

They walked past the locker rooms, and Joel remembered hiding out there his rookie year when a tornado had come through the city. The building had gone through an extensive remodel since that time, both for architectural and security purposes. But for a long while, it had been just a place to stow his stuff and hang out before his shift upstairs. But that was about to change. He wanted to get back out into the world and be a cop again. Maybe he wasn't ready for the pressure and isolation that came with undercover work. But he could be a detective. He could run an investigation. He could help Mollie.

He followed A.J. into the empty elevator and waited for the doors to close before he spoke. "I talked to Mollie Crane last night. She does have evidence against August Di Salvo."

"Yeah? She tell you what she has on him?"

This was where Joel needed to tread carefully. "It sounds like something in a file or on a flash drive. She took it to blackmail Di Salvo into signing their divorce papers."

Although his posture looked relaxed as he leaned against the back railing of the elevator, A.J.'s full attention was zeroed in on Joel. "She gonna work with us?"

Joel shook his head. "Mollie is in a very vulnerable position. I don't know if we should continue working this investigation through her. There has to be another avenue we can pursue."

"We tried that already. We couldn't get any witnesses to stick to their original testimony against him. His attorney, Kyra Schmidt, got him off on time served and a fine for obstruction of justice. We need hard evidence and a reliable witness."

Imagining Mollie up on the witness stand while Di Salvo stared daggers at her, and Kyra Schmidt glibly made her look like she was too scared to know her own mind, wasn't an easy picture to stomach. "If she turns it over to us, what's to stop him from going after her? He's threatened to kill her more than once. She claims it's her only leverage to keep him out of her life."

A.J. straightened as they neared the third floor. "Keep him out of her life? What do you think the car in that alley and the break-in at her apartment are about? I'd say Di Salvo or someone who works for him is back in her life already."

The elevator stopped, and Joel followed A.J. through the check-in desk and cubicles of detectives to reach his office in the back hallway. "Those are the angles I want to pursue. If we can tie either one of those crimes back to Di Salvo, we can at least get an arrest warrant and get that guy off the streets so she can breathe a little easier."

A.J. unlocked his door and invited Joel to one of the chairs in front of his desk while the supervising officer circled around to his own chair. "You're going to need a lot more than a B&E and reckless endangerment to keep a Di Salvo behind bars."

"But if we have more than just what she brings to the investigation, doesn't that lessen the threat to her?"

A.J. eyed him for a moment before sitting. "How close are you getting to her?"

"She's staying at my house."

"You up for a protection detail like that?"

Joel paced to the window and looked down on the parking lot below. He scrubbed his hand over the trimmed stubble on his chin that he'd decided against shaving off completely this morning because Mollie had said she liked how it felt against her skin when he'd kissed her last night. He considered A.J.'s question. Clearly, his emotions and desire were already getting tangled up with Mollie Crane.

But was he ready to put his life on the line to save someone he cared about again? His heart would do anything to protect her. But his brain wasn't so sure he was the best man for the job. "I don't know, A.J. I've been sittin' a desk for a few months now. That's why I was at the shooting range this afternoon. I know there's a gap between being fit for duty, and being fit enough to hold my own on the street the way I used to."

"Maybe you're a step slower than you used to be. Or you hurt more at the end of a long day. But you were one of my best operatives out on the streets. A lot of people are serving time because of the work you've done. Even the cowards who tried to kill you. You can think on your feet. You're aware of everything going on around you. You know when to hide, when to run, and when to fight." A.J.'s dark eyes drilled into Joel's gaze, making sure he understood what the veteran detective was saying to him. "Even beat-up around the edges, you're a good cop. You need to own that."

Joel returned to his seat across from A.J. He braced his forearms on his knees and clasped his hands together. "The instincts are still there, but I find myself second-guessing almost every decision I make. I'm not sure I know who to trust. I'm not sure I even trust myself."

"Let your training get you past those doubts. You trust me?"

"Yes, sir."

"Then I'll be your handler. I'll get you whatever you need as fast as I can." A.J. picked up the phone on his desk, as if he was about to make a call and get the ball rolling on him becoming an active investigator again. "You trust Mollie?"

Joel hesitated.

A.J.'s thumb ended the call before it had even connected. "It's your decision. You want me to assign someone else to work the case? To protect her?" He leaned back in his chair. "I think Rocky Garner's available."

"That's a low blow." He pushed himself upright. His boss probably wouldn't be giving him a hard time on this if he didn't think he could handle himself successfully.

"Think on it, Joel. Until Miss Crane decides to give us and the D.A. a statement on this evidence she has, Di Salvo will always be a threat to her. What if she decides never to let us help her nail her ex? Can you be on alert 24/7 the rest of your life?"

"If that's what she needs."

"You have to sleep sometime. You're gonna need some backup." A.J. pointed the phone at him, sending the message that even though he was supportive of his team, he was still the man in charge. "I'd have a lot easier time budgeting the extra manpower with the brass if we were getting useful intel from her."

Joel leaned back in his chair, still needing some time to make his decision. "What did you and Josh and the crime lab determine about the break-in at Mollie's apartment?"

"I believe it was as much about intimidation as it was finding this evidence you say she has. It wasn't just a search—it was personal. No more written threats, but…"

Joel wasn't sure he wanted to hear the details, but he needed to. "But what?"

"The intruder went through her lingerie and shredded it. A picture of an old woman with Miss Crane had been cut up, too."

"Her granny?" Joel cursed. "He's trying to break her. He's trying to get in her head and punish her for having the strength and resourcefulness to outwit him and play hardball with him so that she could get away from the family." The only time he'd seen an obsession like the one Di Salvo had for Mollie was when he witnessed Cici's addiction to drugs firsthand. The thing he wanted the most—to hurt Mollie—was the most important thing in his life. "He probably believes that if he can victimize her again, make her afraid, he can force her to give up the evidence and stop anything incriminating from getting to us and the D.A."

"You think her ex can break her with his intimidation tactics?"

"No. She's a strong woman. I just don't think she always believes it."

"Sounds like somebody else I know, *amigo*." A.J.'s dark eyes narrowed with a piercing stare before he waved him on his way. "Now, get out of here so I can get some work done."

Joel rose from his chair and crossed to the door. He paused with his hand on the doorknob. "May I ask a question?" A.J. nodded. "I heard that you went undercover with your wife, before you married her. Because she was a witness to a murder?"

"That's right." A.J.'s gaze drifted to the picture on his desk of his wife and two boys. "Claire and I met when I was working that case. She was the only person who could identify the hit man."

"Would you have trusted her protection to anyone else but you?"

"That was a different situation. She was already under my skin, and I was falling in love with her. It was my honor and my duty to protect her."

"Would you put her life in anyone else's hands?"

Dark eyes studied his. "No." Then A.J. opened a file and

picked up his phone, already going back to work. "Talk to her. See if you can get her to open up to you. And watch your back out there." Knowing he was dismissed, Joel nodded, stepped out, and closed the door.

Under his skin and falling in love. That was exactly where he stood with Mollie.

His decision was made.

JOEL ENJOYED THE training session with Magnus and Mollie. And now, as he watched Jessie and Garrett Caldwell's foster son, Nate, play with Magnus and a myriad of other dogs of all sizes and breeds—from a lumbering Newfoundland to an active Jack Russell terrier, who was darting amongst the other dogs in search of the balls the boy was throwing—he could see the benefits of having a pet or partnering with a working dog.

He drank a long swallow of the tea Jessie had served to the four adults watching the dogs and boy play from the back deck. "Man, I miss having dogs around." He took a seat in the Adirondack chair next to Mollie and pressed the icy glass to his forehead to cool off from the ninety-degree heat. "I wish I could bottle that work drive. I would have graduated from physical therapy and been cleared for active duty a month sooner if I could have focused like Magnus does."

"You recently suffered a trauma, too, Detective Standage?" Jessie asked.

Back to reality. His lighthearted mood vanished. He'd been treating this early evening session like a date when he should have been thinking about how to move the Di Salvo investigation forward while keeping Mollie safe.

The thick, humid air weighed heavy in his lungs as he

took in a deep breath and set his drink down. "Yeah. I was injured in the line of duty."

Garrett Caldwell was still wearing his Jackson County deputy's uniform since he'd gotten home from work just before the training session had ended. "Sorry to hear that. What happened?"

Mollie reached over and squeezed Joel's hand. He was grateful for the gentle touch and lightly curled his fingers around hers. Jessie noticed the contact, too. Since he'd figured out that these training sessions were like therapy for Mollie, he wanted to help her get the answers she needed about Magnus. That meant opening up about himself, too, apparently. Still, he opted for sharing the barest of bare-bones versions of his story. "I was working undercover. Got made as a cop."

"That's rough," Garrett sympathized. Judging by the silver in his hair and the chevrons on his badge, he'd had considerable experience in law enforcement. He understood the dangers a man with a badge faced when meeting the enemy face-to-face.

But Jessie wanted details. "What else?"

Joel pinned her with a look. That woman was as intuitive about reading people as she was dogs, it seemed. He must have been staring at her for too long because Garrett moved to sit on the arm of the chair beside his wife and drape a protective arm around her shoulders. "Jessie's just trying to understand the complete picture so she can make an accurate assessment of what's going on with Magnus."

"Sorry." His grip pulsed around Mollie's, and his raw feelings settled to a manageable level with that simple connection to cling to. "I was betrayed by my last girlfriend. She set me up with her dealer. Told him I was a cop."

Mollie leaned forward to add, "She's gone, too. Drug overdose. Joel tried to save her."

A stark look temporarily darkened Garrett's gray eyes, and he leaned down to kiss Jessie on the crown of her hair. The older woman's hand squeezed her husband's knee, and she gazed up at him until he nodded, and the fiercely protective expression finally eased. "Yeah. Drug dealers can be tough SOBs to deal with."

Joel nodded, thinking Garrett and Jessie and possibly that little boy they were both studying so tenderly now had some personal experience with a drug dealer. Jessie inadvertently confirmed it when she looked up at her husband. "They're okay now, Garrett. Just remember, Nate and Abby are going to truly be ours by Christmas."

"Damn right, they are." He tipped Jessie's chin up and kissed her gently on the mouth. Then he stood, apparently satisfied that his wife was safe without him beside her. He pointed to the house. "I'm just going to check to make sure Abby and her puppy are doing okay upstairs." Joel stood when the older man extended his hand. "Good to meet you, Detective. Mollie."

After he'd gone into the house to see to their foster daughter, Jessie smiled. "Garrett's such a protective father. That little girl isn't going to be allowed to date until she's well into her thirties if he has his way."

Joel smiled as he was meant to, although he felt a little lost when Mollie released his hand. Jessie stood and invited both of them to join her at the railing to watch the dogs eagerly chase the balls and bring them back to the boy, who rewarded them with pets and praise and throwing the balls again. "So, what's the verdict, ma'am?" Joel asked. "Magnus seemed to work just as well with me as he did Mollie, once she showed me the commands. Am I a bad influence on the dog? Am I preventing him from helping her?"

"I don't think so. Mollie, you said Magnus stayed by your side when you had the break-in?"

She nodded. "And he growled at the man who made me feel so uncomfortable."

Jessie tilted her gaze to Joel. "And Magnus came to comfort you when you were telling your story to Mollie."

"That's right."

Jessie pulled her long, blond braid from her shoulder and tossed it behind her back. "I think I know what's going on."

"Please tell me," Mollie urged.

"Magnus sees Joel as part of your pack, and he's protecting the pack," Jessie explained. "Mals are overachievers. Why just take care of one human when he can take care of two? He sees the two of you together as a unit he's in charge of. Basically, he wants to be a service dog for you both. He wants to please you both. I hope you two are serious because he thinks you are."

"Serious?" Mollie echoed. "Like a couple?"

"Yes."

Joel reached down to capture her hand again and lifted it to his lips to kiss it, taking a moment to rub his chin across the back of her hand, giving her some of those hundred little caresses she'd liked so well last night. Her blue eyes darkened, and her lips parted with a sharp intake of breath. Yeah, that kiss last night hadn't been a fluke. These feelings that were hitting him hard and fast seemed to be mutual. "We're working on it."

Mollie's gaze locked on to his. "We are. We have some issues we're still working through, but I care a great deal about Joel."

"Ditto."

She rolled her eyes in that beautifully snarky way she had at his eloquent response, but she was smiling. Then she looked out at Magnus charging across the yard to reach the ball first. "So, you think he's okay? There's nothing wrong with him?"

Jessie shook her head. "I'd keep up your regular training—both of you now. And let him do his job. I think he'll continue to alert when you have a panic attack and—" Jessie glanced up at Joel "—he'll offer you comfort when you're stressed about work or events in your past. And he'll probably be protective of you both."

"Okay. Then I'll try not to worry." Mollie stepped in front of Joel and embraced the other woman. "Thank you, Jessie. I was so worried that either I was a failure or Magnus was."

Joel settled his hand at the small of Mollie's back as they hugged, letting his fingertips slide beneath the T-shirt she wore to touch a strip of soft skin above the waistband of her jeans. Mollie didn't flinch at the modest contact, and since she seemed okay with it, he didn't pull away. But they'd just crossed an emotional hurdle by admitting they cared about each other, and he needed to touch her as much as she needed to hug the woman who had given her a way out of constant fear and stress with Magnus.

"No way is either of you a failure." Jessie smiled, and he was pleased to see Mollie smiling back as the women parted. He was even more pleased to feel Mollie slide her arm behind his waist and hook her thumb into the belt loop of his jeans. "You just have a very smart dog," Jessie continued. "You know, sometimes, I think with his hearing loss, that Magnus feels broken, and he feels he has to do more—be more—to prove that he's important and loved and necessary."

"I understand that," Mollie said, surprising Joel. "I think that's why the two of us bonded."

"You're not losing that bond," Jessie assured her, squeezing Joel's arm to include him. "You're just enriching it by adding Joel to your pack."

Was she talking about dogs or his relationship with Mollie now?

Mollie seemed to ponder the same question for a few seconds before she pulled away and gave Jessie another quick hug. "We'd better get going. It's dinnertime and you have hungry children to feed. Thanks so much."

Jessie frowned. "This isn't the last time I'm seeing you, is it?"

"Of course not. You and your family have a standing invitation at Pearl's Diner. I make to-die-for milkshakes that your kids will love."

"I'd love one, too."

Mollie nodded toward the aging German shepherd mix that had been napping by Jessie's chair. "And bring Shadow with you. Service dogs are welcome there."

"I will."

"Magnus! Come!" Although the Newfoundland had tired of playtime and lain down in the middle of the yard, the other dogs were running circles around him and Nate.

When the Belgian Malinois didn't immediately respond to Mollie's summons, Joel thrust his tongue against his teeth and let out an ear-piercing whistle. The dogs all stopped and turned as one. "Magnus!" Joel put two fingers down at his side, and the black-and-tan dog came running right to him. He touched his wet nose to Joel's fingers, then sat beside him, heavily panting from his exertion. When he saw Mollie crossing her arms and glaring up at him, he quickly apologized. "I didn't think he heard you."

"I can see we're going to have to work on exactly who the pack leader is," Mollie teased before handing him the dog's harness and leash.

Jessie laughed along with Joel. "As long as it isn't Magnus, you two will be okay. Come on, I'll walk you out to your truck."

Chapter Nine

Following another round of goodbyes and a promise to keep in touch, Joel pulled his truck past the gated entrance and security cameras and turned out onto the road leading to Highway 40 into Kansas City. Since there was no center console on the wide bench seat of his truck, Magnus was stretched out between him and Mollie, resting his head on Mollie's lap. She stroked her left hand along the dog's back, more out of habit, he hoped, than any nervousness she was feeling about being alone with him again.

He waited at the light before turning onto the highway. Because they were headed into Kansas City, they were driving against the rush hour traffic heading out to the countryside and small towns east of the city. And since 40 was a divided highway out here in the county, they were pretty much the only vehicle on their side heading west.

He replayed the words she'd said to Jessie. *I care a great deal about Joel.*

Ditto might not have been the snappiest response, but he meant it. He cared a great deal about Mollie. And he had an idea that Magnus had spotted right away what the two of them had been reluctant to recognize, much less act on. He and Mollie meant something to each other. And if she gave him the chance, they were going to mean something to each other for a long time to come—maybe for the rest of their lives.

But he'd start small. He had a feeling knowing when to be patient and when to push would be key to any long-term relationship with Mollie. "Speaking of dinner…" Not the smoothest start to a conversation, but he had Mollie's attention. "We'll drive past about any kind of fast-food restaurant you want when we get to K.C. We can drive through one of them and get dinner to eat at home. Are you in the mood for anything in particular?"

"You're not going to zap something in the microwave for me and show off your cooking prowess?"

He loved it when she teased him. It felt healthy. Normal. A special way to communicate between just the two of them. "Nah. I'm saving that for our third or fourth date. I don't want to spoil you."

She laughed with him. "So, we're dating now?"

Joel sobered up, not wanting any misunderstanding between them. "I'd like to. Maybe I just needed Jessie to put things into perspective for me, but I like you, Moll. A lot."

"You said that last night."

"Yeah, well, maybe it's more than a lot." He glanced across the cab to find her listening intently to his words. "When you told Jessie you cared about me, something seemed to click inside." He skimmed the rearview mirror and took note of a couple of cars on the highway behind them before turning his focus to the road in front of them. "Even when you were still married to the jackass who hurt you, I was attracted to you."

"I was black-and-blue, and I had a split lip and cracked rib."

"You were glorious. Strong. Brave. Not afraid to set me straight when you told me the rules of the house." He glanced her way again. "Di Salvo would have made things worse for you if I had tried to help you then, wouldn't he."

"Yes. He would have hurt you, too. If not physically, you'd have lost your job, for sure. Of course, I didn't know then that chauffeuring wasn't your real job."

"I was involved with Cici then, so I wouldn't have acted on my attraction. I felt guilty for not being able to help you then, but I admired you." She turned away to look out the side window, and he took note of the SUV behind them, slowing and turning left into a tire and auto repair business between the east and west lanes of the highway. With the hills, curves, and trees along the highway, there was only one other vehicle in sight behind them, and that one disappeared into a valley, and they were alone again. "Then I met you again that night at the diner when Rocky Garner put his hands on you, and I was struck all over again by how much I was attracted to you. I wanted to punch his lights out for upsetting you like that."

"I was a mess, Joel," she reminded him. "I'm still a bit of a mess."

He shook his head. "You're a work in progress. So am I. We've both been through some stuff, but we're getting better. The chemistry between us gets my blood pumping, just like it always has. You mentioned that you miss human contact. But when you hold my hand or reach out to me, it soothes something inside me. Knowing you trust me enough to be the man you can do normal, touchy-feely stuff with makes me feel like a stud."

She chuckled at that description. "You *are* a stud, Joel Standage."

He tried to explain himself in a way that didn't make him sound so egotistical. "Spending time with you makes me feel better about myself. I feel grounded. You settle things inside me."

"We're comfortable with each other."

"Yeah. I think *comfortable* for us means we're good for each other. Maybe I sensed that potential bond when we first met two years ago." He shifted his grip on the wheel, wishing he wasn't doing so much of the talking here. "Please tell me I'm not the only one feeling this connection between us."

"You're not," she answered quietly.

"We're both free of our exes now, in one way or another. We can do something about how we feel."

"I'm not free of Augie."

"You can be."

He heard her pained gasp above the hum of the truck's tires on the pavement. "If I turn over what I know to you and KCPD."

"Think about it, Moll. If we could get him behind bars where he belongs, and you've got the evidence to keep him there, then you'd be free of him. His parents are only going to bail him out so many times. His lawyer can't charm a judge or dispute hard evidence. His so-called business associates won't let the Di Salvos touch another dime of their money if he goes to prison." He remembered her vindictive wish from last night. "They might not want him alive in prison if they think he's going to turn state's evidence and implicate them in exchange for a lighter sentence."

Magnus whined in her lap now, and Joel hated that he was causing Mollie any kind of distress. "What about those weeks or months between handing over the flash drive that got me out of that house and testifying against him? He'll kill me, Joel. Or he or his father will hire someone to do it for him. Then you've got no witness, and Kyra Schmidt can refute or discredit any evidence you got through me, and I'll still be dead."

He wanted to reach across the seat and be the one she turned to when she needed comfort. But he kept his hands on the wheel and let Magnus do his job.

"I'd be with you the whole time. We'd go to a safe house. There'd be backup in place. A.J., Josh, a SWAT team. Whatever we need to get you through the trial and sentencing. I'll keep you safe. If you'll let me." He took a deep breath and put his heart on the line. "I want a future with you. We can move as slowly as you need to, and I'm okay with that, I swear. As long as I know you want that future, too."

"I do." Her words were hushed, but he heard them loud and clear. "But I'm scared, Joel. So much."

Her blue eyes were hard to look away from to concentrate on his driving. "You think I'm not scared? I lost everything once. But I'm falling in love with you, and I don't want to give up without fighting for us."

"You want me to fight for us, too." It was a statement, not a question.

"Can you? Will you give us a chance?"

She considered his challenge for several seconds. "Will you give me some time to think about it?"

The volume of his sigh of relief was almost embarrassing. Magnus's tail thumped against his thigh, and he considered it a good sign. "I'll give you as much time as you need—"

His gaze caught a blur of movement in the rearview mirror, and he swore. How the hell had that car caught up to them so fast? The driver must be breaking all kinds of speed limits.

And then it topped the hill behind them.

"Son of a…"

"Joel?"

Black Lexus. Gold trim. A dent in its fancy grill from where it had bounced over a curb at high speed.

He pushed a little harder on the accelerator, needing to put some distance between them. "Moll, are you buckled up?"

"Of course."

"Magnus is in his harness, secured in the seat?"

"Yes." Those questions naturally made her suspicious. "What's wrong?"

"We're being followed. I know that car and he's gaining speed." She whipped around to look behind them, but he urged her to face forward again. "Don't look. I don't want to alert him that we're onto him yet." He nodded toward her door. "Check your side-view mirror."

She looked out her window and sat up straighter. "That's the same car that tried to run us down in the alley. What is he doing?"

He tightened his grip on the steering wheel and channeled every bit of training he'd had into doing what was necessary to get them out of what he suspected was about to happen. "Any chance you can get a read on the license plate?"

"Uh. It's a Missouri Bicentennial plate, with the red and blue squiggly lines?" Her fingers curled beneath Magnus's harness, and she braced her other hand against the dashboard to steady herself as they picked up speed to peer more closely into the mirror. "He's coming up awfully fast." She glanced back at Joel. "How fast can this old truck go?"

"This old truck can outrun that engine he's got any day of the week. He looks stylish, but I've got substance."

"That's right. You fix engines."

"Can't cook an omelet like that one you made this morning, but I can make this baby run like a Mack truck."

Their words came out faster and louder as they raced up one hill and down another. She leaned over Magnus and rested her fingers on his forearm. "I like substance."

"Me, too, babe. License plate."

"M-X—I don't know if that's a three or an eight." They hit a bump and all three left their seats for a split second. "I lost him behind that hill."

"Grab my phone off my belt." He gave her the security code to unlock it. "Find A.J. in my contacts. Give him our location, the three digits you got off the plate, and tell him we're being pursued." Joel swore as the car reappeared behind them. He couldn't make out the driver through the sun reflecting off the windshield, but he could see the arm and the gun sliding out the driver's side window. "Tell him there's going to be shots fired."

"What?"

"Do it!"

He nudged Magnus's butt to get him to sit up and move over, and Mollie curled her arm around him while she rattled off information to A.J. like a seasoned dispatcher. "He's sending backup and calling the sheriff's department. Says he's not clear on jurisdiction."

"Tell him to notify Garrett Caldwell." They sank into their seats at the bottom of the next hill before the truck kicked into a stronger gear and flew up the next hill. "We may need a friend to smooth things over for us because this is about to go down outside city limits."

He saw the first flash of a gunshot and knew the driver had fired his weapon. They were going too fast to get an accurate aim—he hoped. Hell. He *heard* the next pop of gunfire and knew the guy was getting too close.

"Shots fired, A.J!" he yelled for his boss to hear. "He's going to try to run us off the road."

"He says 'Affirmative.'"

Lowering his voice, he risked sliding his hand over hers where she clung to Magnus. "You okay?"

"No. I'm scared out of my mind. But I'll do whatever you tell me." She checked her side-view mirror again a split second before a bullet shattered the reflection. She jerked back in her seat. "Joel!"

He eyed the road up ahead. This guy had a plan. But Joel was onto his game. He had a plan, too. "He waited for this straight, empty stretch of road. We need to do this before we hit that curve at the end and those trees up ahead."

"Do what?"

"Hang up. Hold on."

"Gotta go." She ended the call and tucked his phone into the front pocket of her jeans. The black car swerved into the left lane and crept up beside his truck. "Damn it." The passenger side window was open. Was there a second shooter in the car? Or was the driver going to pull the incredibly foolish stunt of shooting through the car at breakneck speed and risk a ricochet inside the vehicle if his aim was off? "Get down!"

"Down, boy." Mollie pulled Magnus down and leaned into the middle of the seat with him while Joel reached for his holster. When he couldn't immediately free his Glock, he felt nimble fingers brush against his and unhook the clasp to free his weapon. "Be careful, Joel."

He breathed deeply—once, twice—then steeled himself for the coming confrontation. "I got this."

Mollie squeezed his thigh. "That's what A.J. said."

And then there was no talking. There was speed and gunfire. The black Lexus drifted onto the far shoulder, then the driver overcorrected and nearly clipped the side of the truck. He heard one ping off the bed of the truck. Another bullet smacked into the door panel. *Damn that loser. He's messin' up my truck!* Mollie gasped as another shot shattered his mirror and he felt the nick of something sharp pierce his forearm. *And you're scaring my woman!*

The truck sat up higher than the Lexus so he couldn't see into to car to know who was shooting. But he knew the guy was firing wild. A stray bullet could come right through his open window if the shooter leaned over far enough to angle his shot up. But that wasn't happening at this speed.

But that also meant *his* shots wouldn't hit their intended target, either.

Plan B. Think on your feet. Know every detail of your surroundings. That's what A.J. said he had over other cops. They were barreling toward the curve and the thick grove of trees beyond. No cars up ahead. No vehicles close behind. What he wouldn't pay to be a lefty right about now. But he could make this work.

"This is gonna be loud," he warned Mollie a split second before he eased up on the accelerator and the black car surged ahead of them. The shooter had actually done him a favor by taking off his side mirror. It made it easier for Joel to twist his body and brace his right hand outside the doorframe. He took a bead on the black car and fired off five shots in rapid succession.

He hit his target with bullet number four.

The right rear tire exploded, sending the Lexus into a tailspin. The car swerved from one side of the road to the other, leaving traces of rubber and sparks from the bare rim on the pavement. When it sailed past the shoulder and hit the ground that had been softened by last night's rain, the car flipped over and rolled three times before it plowed into the trunk of one of the stately pine trees that had been planted ages ago when Highway 40 was still a two-lane road.

Joel pumped his brakes to a stop and pulled off onto the side of the highway, turning on his warning blinkers before he shut off the engine. He ripped off his seat belt and holstered his gun before reaching down to palm the back of Mollie's head. "You can sit up now, babe. Are you okay?" She was pale and breathing hard as she pushed herself upright, but Mollie nodded. Spine of steel, this woman. He spared a quick scratch around the ears for Magnus. "How about the big guy?"

"He's fine. We're both fine." She reached up to cup the side of his jaw. "Are you okay?" Then she saw the blood trickling down his forearm. "Joel!" She grabbed his wrist and pulled it across his lap to inspect the small cut. "You *are* hurt."

"It's just a scratch." He could barely feel the sting with her hands moving so tenderly around the injury.

"No more bullet holes or shrapnel wounds, okay?"

He wished he could make her that promise.

"First aid kit?"

"Under the front seat. I'm good for now," he assured

her, pulling her fingers from his arm. "Can't say the same for my truck, but I can fix that. I need to check the other driver."

She'd been so helpful in following his orders when he needed to keep her safe, that she hadn't seen the devastating crash. But she saw the aftermath. Her fingers went to the locket that hung inside her shirt and she whispered a soft prayer. Gouges of sod were torn up along the car's tumbling path. Scratches of silver bled through the black paint. A headlamp and part of the grill had snapped off and were scattered along with a hubcap and shreds of the rubber tire in a debris field. Steam or smoke was spilling out from the crumpled hood.

There was no sign of the driver. But whether he was unable to get out of the car, or he was lying in wait to shoot them, Joel couldn't know until he got eyes on the perp.

He was relieved to see the color flooding back into her cheeks. "Should I call 9-1-1?"

Joel nodded. "Backup is already on the way, but we'll also need an ambulance and someone to reroute traffic around the accident."

"I can do that."

He massaged the back of her neck and let his fingers tangle in the curls of her hair for a moment before releasing her. "Stay in the truck with Magnus."

She pulled out his phone and handed it back to him before unbuckling and pulling her own phone from the back pocket of her jeans. "We're good, too."

Taking the woman at her word, Joel opened his door. His gun was in his hands, and he was carefully making his way to the wrecked vehicle.

"KCPD! Drop your weapon and put your hands out the

window where I can see them." He should have put on the protective vest he kept in his go bag in the back of the truck. But he hadn't planned on making a traffic stop today. And this guy—this loser—was definitely stopped. With the tinted windows in the back still intact, he steeled himself for approaching the car. "KCPD! I said to get your hands…"

The last of his adrenaline whooshed out on a frustrated curse. The driver wasn't lying in wait to shoot him. The driver wasn't doing anything ever again.

He identified the location of the man's gun on the floor in front of the passenger's seat. Then he holstered his own weapon and reached in to press his fingers against the man's neck. The driver had been battered around inside the car. The blows to the head or even his chest smacking against the steering wheel would have been enough to stop his heart.

Joel wasn't sure if he was angry or saddened by the loss of life. It had been a damn foolish stunt to try to pull off. But he needed to know why this particular man had been targeting Mollie.

He spared a moment to reach inside the car and turn off the engine before stalking back to his pickup. He opened the door on Mollie's side of the truck and held out his hand for her phone. "We're not getting any answers out of him."

"I'm handing you over to Detective Standage, ma'am," Mollie explained to the Dispatcher before surrendering her phone. "He's dead?"

Joel nodded. He requested to be patched through to Deputy Caldwell. He was amused, and stunned again by Mollie's determination, to see her open the first aid kit to clean and doctor the cut on his arm while he talked on the phone.

Once he explained the situation to the deputy sheriff, he felt a shade better about what he needed to ask of Mollie. "Thanks, Garrett. I'll see what I can find out. See you in a few. Standage out."

Joel waited in the open triangle between the open door and the body of the truck while she taped gauze over the cut and tucked her phone back into her jeans. "Jessie's Garrett is coming?"

"We're still in the county. We're not in KCPD's jurisdiction. But I want someone I know backing us up on scene." Perched on the seat above him, Mollie had watched him through the entire conversation. He braced his palms on the seat on either side of her thighs. "How squeamish are you?"

Her eyes got wide, then narrowed with a question. "After surviving Augie? Not much."

"Any triggers?"

"A few." She looked beyond him to the car and understood what he was really asking. "If you're worried about a lot of blood, though, I'll be okay."

"I really need you to confirm the ID on this guy."

"Is it Augie?"

Joel shook his head. But if he was right, she wasn't going to like what he'd found.

"Can I take Magnus?"

"Yes. And you'll take me."

"Then I'll be fine."

She scooted to the edge of the seat to climb out the door, but he stopped her and planted a quick, firm kiss on her lips. "Bravest woman I've ever met."

Her gaze skimmed across his face, his shoulders, and chest, before blue eyes met his. "Kiss me again, Joel."

Although he was surprised by the request, he didn't hesitate to tunnel his fingers into her hair and lean in to cover her mouth with his. Her taste was sweet. Her touch was tender. And Joel knew he'd never shared a kiss that meant as much to him as these few stolen moments of shared support did. She stroked his face as she pulled away. "This grounds me, too," she whispered. Then she braced her other hand against his bicep and climbed down. "Magnus, come."

He waited for the dog to take his place beside her, then captured her hand in his and led them to the wreck.

When they reached the passenger side of the crumpled vehicle, Joel took her by the shoulders and turned her to look at him a moment. "Take a deep breath." She did. "It's not pretty. Looks like he hit his head more than once."

"You're positive he'd dead?"

More than. "Yeah, babe."

Mollie inhaled another deep breath before she stepped up to the driver's window. She quickly spun away and buried her nose against his chest. "Oh, my."

Joel willingly wrapped his arms around her and pulled her farther away from the body. "Tell me that's who I think it is."

Shock seemed to chase away her fear when she looked up at him. "Rocky Garner. He's not in uniform, but that's him."

"There's been some bad blood between him and me, so I didn't want to make the identification. And I'm not touching the body until the M.E. gets here."

"Garner's been after me? I mean he's a jerk, but... trying to kill me? Us? That doesn't make any sense. Can a cop even afford a car like this?"

Joel pointed to the sticker on the rear window. "It's a rental. Stay here." He circled around to reach through the open window of the passenger door. He pulled the rental

Chapter Ten

Mollie awoke to a cold nose nudging her hand, followed by a whine and several warm licks across her skin.

It wasn't the first time Magnus had awakened her in the middle of the night. But it was the first time she hadn't been in the throes of a nightmare when he forced her out of her horrific memories and fear that sometimes never left her, even when she slept.

The moment her eyes opened, Magnus crawled up on the bed beside her and licked her cheek. He was whimpering in earnest now, and Mollie wondered if she'd been dreaming something awful and had simply forgotten it the moment she was awake. Only she wasn't covered in a cold sweat, and she wasn't shaking with the terror that usually accompanied the panic attacks that could take hold of her even in her sleep.

She sat up to embrace the dog. His eyes were almost invisible in the blackness of his face and the darkness of the room, but she could feel his strength and warmth and smell his treat-scented breath. "I'm okay, good boy. Mama's okay. Did I scare you? What's wrong?"

And then she heard the headboard in Joel's bedroom thump against the wall of the guest room where she slept.

This time she did startle and jumped to the middle of the bed. "What the…?"

She petted Magnus, timing her breaths to each stroke and slowing both until she was fully oriented in the bedroom that was illuminated only by the bathroom light Joel had left on for her across the hall. Her sweats had been pushed up to her knees and the long sleeves of her T-shirt were nearly up to her elbows. Maybe she'd gotten hot during the night, or maybe she had been unsettled in her sleep.

But when the headboard thumped against the wall again and Magnus woofed, she knew she wasn't the one in distress tonight. The dog gently mouthed her hand, urging her to move. Someone less accustomed to violence and nightmares might have thought she was overhearing the sounds of sex. But she was far too attuned to the insidious ways fear could overtake one when they were at their most vulnerable in sleep.

"I'm coming. I'm coming." She pushed Magnus off the bed and scooted to the edge. She shivered when she stepped onto the cool wood beyond the small rug and blanket where she'd been sleeping. Tugging her sleeves down to her wrists and smoothing her pants down her legs, she put her hand on Magnus's head and followed him down the hall to Joel's room. "Show me."

Magnus led her unerringly through the shadows to the open door of Joel's bedroom. She stopped to let her eyes adjust to the near total darkness. "Magnus!" she called in as loud a whisper as she could without disturbing Joel.

Instead of sitting next to her when she stopped, the dog trotted into the room and propped his front paws on the bed. He dodged and dropped to the floor when Joel kicked his foot out from the covers twisted around his legs, but he had his paws right back up on the bed a moment later. Magnus wasn't the only one concerned about the man who was thrashing in his sleep as though his life depended on it. Besides the sounds of him twisting in the bed and pummeling his pillows, she could hear guttural vocal sounds coming from his throat that nearly broke her heart. That had been her more nights than she could count.

"No. Stop." Those words and her name were words she could make out.

But it was the strangled whimpers that had her whispering his name from the doorway. "Joel?"

Magnus trotted back to her and tugged at her sleeve again. Not sure exactly what she was supposed to do in this situation, she listened to her heart instead of all the damaged memories in her head. She let Magnus pull her into the room. "Good boy. You're Mama's good boy."

She cautiously approached the bed and raised her volume to something more than a whisper. "Joel."

She turned on the lamp beside the bed, blinking against its soft illumination. Wow. Joel Standage, in the middle of summer, at least, slept in nothing but a pair of gym shorts. And with the covers down around his ankles, she could see every inch of muscle across his chest, and the whole of the tattoo circling down his left arm. He had an innie belly button and those V-shaped muscles at his hips that pointed down to that most masculine part of him. Mollie gulped at the hard beauty of his body and felt an answering heat of feminine awareness between her thighs and at the tips of her breasts. How could this man ever call himself *forgettable*?

And how had she ever believed that she'd never be at-

tracted to a man again? Her body, her heart—and her dog—
kept drawing her toward this one.

But hearing the keening sound in his throat and watching
him clench every muscle in his body against the terrors in
his mind shook her out of her hormonal stupor. "Joel," she
called in a louder, firmer tone. Still no response. But she
knew who had a stronger voice. "Magnus, speak!"

At the same time Magnus barked, Mollie touched Joel's
shoulder. "Joel—"

Suddenly Joel was awake. She screeched in surprise
when he snatched her wrist and flipped her beneath him
on the bed. Her breath lodged in her chest at the weight of
him crushing her, the feel of her wrists cinched within his
grip and his hips cradled intimately against hers. She knew
a brief moment of panic. But that awareness was followed
just as quickly by the realization that she wasn't caught in
a bruising grip, and there were certainly no insults or pro-
fanities being hurled at her. *Not Augie. Not Augie.* "Joel?"

Those golden eyes blinked, then opened wide in horror.

She inhaled a deep breath as Joel scrambled off her.
"Damn, Mollie. I'm so sorry. Did I hurt you?"

"Startled me." She slowly sat up, curling her legs beneath
her. "But I'm okay. I'm more worried about you."

He slid to the edge of the bed, his head bent, elbows on
his knees, his fingers raking through his short hair. "I had
you pinned under me. I didn't bruise your wrists, did I?"

His voice sounded as agonized as those senseless mut-
ters in his throat had.

"I'm okay."

"I didn't remind you of him, did I?" His tortured gaze
sought out hers.

No. No way could this rough-around-the-edges man

with the sense of humor and addictive variety of kisses ever remind her of the cold polish and selfish evil of August Di Salvo.

She scooted to the edge of the bed beside him. She caught the wrist closest to her to pull his hand from the punishing assault on his head. He flinched with the instinct to pull away, but he purposely relaxed his arm against his thigh as if he might hurt her by struggling, and she kept hold of him. She reached out with her left hand to cup his stubbled jaw and turn his anguished face to her. "Joel. Look at me. Take a deep breath. I'm okay."

He did as she asked, much the same way he'd calmed her in the past. "I'm sorry I woke you. I never want to add to your stress."

"You woke Magnus. He was worried about you and came to get me." He glanced down at the dog trying to wedge himself between Mollie and Joel's knees. Mollie moved her hand to the middle of Joel's back and rubbed what she hoped were soothing circles there. "Do you think I'd feel better knowing you were in here suffering, fighting some demon in your sleep, all alone? Magnus did what he was supposed to do. He sensed you were in trouble, and when he couldn't take care of you, he went and got help."

"But *I'm* supposed to be taking care of *you*."

"No. You're supposed to be *protecting* me. And I do feel safe with you. But I'm not an invalid, Joel." She kept one hand on Joel's back—his broad, smooth, incredibly warm back—and petted Magnus with the other. "One of the things I like about you is that you treat me like a normal woman. I've had some experience with nightmares, and I'm a terrific listener. I *am* someone who can help. Please let me. Now praise your buddy here. He did his job."

Joel reluctantly reached down and scrubbed the dog around his ears and muzzle. "Good boy, Magnus. Good boy." Magnus's tail thumped against the floor at the bit of roughhousing. She was relieved to see the hint of a smile at the corner of Joel's mouth. It reached the other corner when Magnus pushed his head into Joel's hands, and they shared some more gentle wrestling. "That's my good boy."

She let the boys bond for a few moments before asking, "Do you need to talk about your dream? It seemed pretty violent."

Joel shook his head. When the wrestling stopped, Magnus stretched out across their feet.

She suspected that Joel appreciated the contact as much as she did. "Should you talk to your therapist about it?"

He glanced at her, then focused on the dog again. "I stopped going."

That might explain why his emotions had manifested themselves in his dreams. "I'm willing to listen to anything you want to tell me. I care when you're hurting like this, but a police psychologist would be able to give you some specific strategies for coping. I talked to a therapist at the shelter where I stayed for a while." She pointed to her canine savior at their feet. "Hence, the service dog. Would you do me a favor and call tomorrow morning to make an appointment?"

He considered her request for a moment, then nodded.

"Thank you."

Joel brushed the backs of his fingers across her cheek and played with her hair, smoothing the tendrils that refused to stay in place off her forehead. While she enjoyed the soft caresses, he seemed to think better of touching her and pulled away. "The nightmare was about you. It was you in that car, battered and bleeding, not Garner. I couldn't save you. Then it was you in that drug house where I found Cici, and they were hurting you." His gravelly voice was raw with emotion. "And then you were in that dumpster with me, and I couldn't save you. I'm going to fail you the same way I failed Cici."

"That's a crock," she muttered. "You *did* save me, Joel. You have saved me. More than once." She pulled her toes from beneath Magnus's warmth and faced Joel, lightly clasping his forearm. "Today on the highway. In that alley. Two years ago when you were undercover. When I was too scared to function, you came, and suddenly I could think again and do what I needed to do. The fact that I'm sitting here with you now and I'm not panicking is a testament to how many times you've saved me. You've given me back the gift of human touch. You've reminded me that I once was a pretty sweet catch."

He folded his larger hand over both of hers. "You still are in my book."

"Nightmares are wicked things, preying on our fears and worries and stress. Our lives haven't been easy. But we're here. And we're both okay." She turned her hand to link her fingers together with his. "Sometimes, you just need the reassurance of someone holding your hand or hugging you or making love, to *feel* that you're safe and cared for. That you're going to be okay."

One eyebrow arched when she said the words *making love*, but he didn't comment on it. "Magnus does that for you. You ground yourself in reality when you pet him or hug him, or he nuzzles his cold nose in your hand."

She smiled at how well he knew her and her dog. "May I do that for you tonight?"

"You want to nuzzle your cold nose in my hand?" His stab at humor reassured her more than anything else that he had recovered from the nightmare and was feeling more like the good man she cared for so deeply.

With that thought foremost in her mind, Mollie asked, "Could I sleep with you and hold you while you sleep?"

"Only if I can hold you, too." He lifted her hand to his lips and gently kissed her fingers. "I'd really love to *feel* that you're safe, even when my mind is trying to tell me otherwise."

Mollie nodded and crawled to the middle of the bed, where she straightened the mess he'd made of his pillows and sheets. Then she lay down and patted the mattress beside her. "Do you have a preference which side you sleep on?"

"The one where you're within arm's reach." He urged her to lie on her left side and snuggled in behind her. With one arm under his head on the pillow, he curled the other arm around her waist. He tugged at the hem of her shirt, and she gasped when she felt his warm, callused fingers splay across her bare skin underneath. "Is this all right?" When she didn't immediately answer, he started to pull his hand from under her shirt. "I'm sorry."

"Don't." Mollie caught his hand and laced her fingers with his to put it right back on her belly and hold him against her. "I like the feel of your hands on me. It's not sex, but this feels intimate to me. I miss intimacy. Lying like this feels good to me."

She felt his lips near the crown of her hair. "Me, too."

They lay together like that, as close as two people who still had their clothes on could be, for several minutes. Mollie felt her own heart rate calm to a contented rhythm, and she relaxed against him, eventually feeling the tension in him begin to fade, too.

Soon after, Joel's voice vibrated against her eardrums. "You know, as much as I love holding you—as much as I need this to settle myself down—I'm having a little trouble with an audience watching us sleep."

Mollie blinked her eyes open to see Magnus resting his head on the bed, those dark, steady orbs indeed watching them. She laughed softly and smiled at the dog. "Give me your hand." She put both their hands on Magnus's head. "Good boy, Magnus. Your pack is safe."

"Good boy," Joel echoed, as they pulled away. "I owe you one, buddy."

"Night-night, Magnus." If a dog could pout, she had a feeling that's what the whiny sound he made meant. "Go night-night, you big goof."

Joel raised his head, and in his firm, gritty tone ordered, "Magnus, night-night."

The dog finally got down, and she could tell by the scratching noises and circling flag of his tail that he was gathering up the throw rug on her side of the bed and making himself a nest to lie down in. Once the dog had obeyed and settled close by, Mollie rolled onto her back and looked up at Joel hovering beside her in the lamplight. She gently poked his chest and chided, "*My* dog, Standage. I don't like that he responds to your commands faster than he does mine."

He captured her hand against his chest, and she felt the heat of his skin branding her. "*Our* dog, Crane. *Our* energetic, overachieving, too-smart-for-his-own-good dog."

She smiled, more than happy to keep her hand pressed against the ticklish dusting of chest hair and the warm skin underneath. "Maybe it means I'm getting better. That taking care of me isn't enough work for him, anymore."

"Are you still willing to go to the Precinct offices tomorrow morning and talk to A.J. and Josh and the assistant district attorney?"

Her nostrils flared with a deep breath, and she dropped her gaze to where her fingers clung to a swell of pectoral muscle. They'd had this conversation in one form or another several times. She'd done her best to make Joel understand the risk she'd be taking by surrendering her evidence against Augie to the ADA. And he'd done his best to make her believe that she would never be alone against the Di Salvo family again. She met Joel's gaze again and nodded. "I haven't made my decision yet. But I'm willing to talk to them. As long as you make that phone call to your therapist in the morning."

"I will. I promise. I need to do better taking care of that part of my recovery."

"Thank you." She raised her head to press her lips against his, rewarding him with a gentle kiss. She lingered when his lips moved tenderly against hers and reached behind his neck to slide her hand across the spiky mess of his hair. He touched his nose to her face and moved his lips along her jawline, inhaling deeply as if he was learning and memorizing her touch and scent. He nipped at her earlobe, and the zing of desire that arrowed down to the juncture of her thighs caught her off guard. Who knew she had an erogenous zone there? After Augie, who knew she had any erogenous zones left?

Sensing her sudden hesitation, if misreading the cause, Joel pulled away and flopped down on his back beside her. "Maybe this isn't a good idea. I can't guarantee that the nightmares won't come back. I'd never hurt you if I was fully conscious. It kills me to think that I could frighten you or be too rough with you when I don't know what I'm doing."

But Mollie wasn't going anywhere. "I'll have Magnus to protect me."

Joel pushed up on his elbow beside her to talk over her and the edge of the bed. "You take my head off if I hurt her in any way, buddy." Magnus answered with a stuttered snore. Laughter vibrated in Joel's chest beneath her hand. "Yeah, that's backup I can count on," he muttered sarcastically. "Still, if I did anything to remind you of him…"

"You don't remind me of him at all." Mollie dropped her voice to a whisper and purposely brushed her lips against his ear. "Augie never liked to cuddle."

She knew Joel got the message behind her words. His eyes glittered with something possessive just before he turned her to her side, slid his arm around her and pulled her into his chest. Her butt nestled into his groin and his legs tangled with hers. "Do you need the covers?"

She shook her head. "You'll keep me warm."

She clutched his forearm between her breasts and sighed at the gentle press of his lips against her hair. "Sleep well, my love."

She smiled at the whispered word and dipped her head to kiss his hand. "You, too."

It was too soon for her to fully believe that she could fall in love again and trust her heart and body to another man. But it wasn't too soon for her to know that when she was ready, it would be with this man.

They fell asleep holding each other, with the cadence of a snoring dog curled up on the rug filling the room with a quiet sense of security.

MOLLIE HAD AWAKENED from the best night's sleep she'd had in ages. The only way she and Joel could have been closer was if they'd been lying skin to skin. And she was surprised to realize that the idea of being with Joel in that way didn't frighten her. She was nervous about being that intimate with any man again, but if the erection pressing against her bottom when she woke hadn't bothered her—and, in fact, had made her feel cherished and desirable—then she had a feeling making love with Joel would be a good experience for her. If he'd enjoyed cuddling so closely with her through the night as much as she had, then she knew he'd be patient with her. Possibly even more patient than she'd be, judging by her own off-the-charts reactions to the man's damn fine body.

But that was this morning, cocooned in the homey sanctuary of Joel's Brookside house, where Joel and Magnus were the only personalities she had to deal with. She trusted both implicitly, and she felt safe with them.

Here, in the tight confines of the Fourth Precinct conference room, surrounded by some heavy hitters in Kansas City law enforcement and the district attorney's office who were analyzing her life and breaking down every detail that could possibly be used against the Di Salvos, she was having a much harder time holding on to that sense of calm and security. It almost felt as if she'd been summoned to a command performance at a Di Salvo dinner party, where she was expected to say certain things and play her part well. Only, these guests weren't talking big bucks and making themselves look good in the worlds of business and culture and KC society. These men and one other woman were strategizing ways to build a case against her ex-husband and redeem the fiasco of the last time they'd gone up against Augie in the courtroom.

There was a big, stocky man in a suit and tie. And though Chief of Police Mitch Taylor's graying hair and authoritative demeanor confirmed that he was the man in charge, he leaned back in his seat at the opposite end of the long, heavy table from her and slowly rubbed his fingers back and forth across his chin while he listened to the intense conversation around the room.

The Black man next to him, Joe Hendricks, was the captain of this Precinct. Apparently, he and the chief were old friends, as he'd been sharing pictures of his grandchildren with Mitch before the meeting started.

The woman, Assistant District Attorney Kenna Parker-Watson, looked like the woman Augie and his parents had tried to transform her into. Straight blond hair. Tall and poised. Her tailored designer suit said she had money, and her pointed comments and quick wit put her on equal footing with the men in the room. She was also happily married, judging by the gold rings on her finger and the smile and kiss she'd shared with a handsome dark-haired detective out in the third floor's main room when she'd arrived.

Of course, she recognized A. J. Rodriguez and Josh Taylor, who was somehow related to the chief of police. She'd missed the exact connection in the flurry of introductions. A.J. was fixated on his laptop on the table in front of him, while Josh paced back and forth, occasionally stopping to jot something on the whiteboard on the wall across from the door.

Joel sat in the chair beside her, doodling pictures on a yellow legal pad and drawing lines from one symbol to the next before scratching the whole thing out, flipping the page and starting the design all over again. Magnus sat in the space between their chairs, his head resting atop her knee. So many big personalities. So much talking. She clung to Magnus's leash and burrowed her fingers into the fur on his warm head. She didn't even care that he was panting, and some drool was trickling down the leg of her jeans and seeping through to her skin.

In fact, she found herself tuning out much of the conversation and focusing on the sound of the dog's breathing and the warmth of him against her when she got too stressed. The air conditioning in the room was working just fine. But Magnus was slightly overheated and panting because he was working so hard to keep her calm.

Joel circled two of the doodles on his paper several times and tapped the pad with his pen sharply enough that she looked over to see what he had drawn. "I found a tracker on my truck when I was checking the damage. There was one on Mollie's car, too. Mine has only been there a few days. It's still shiny new. Hers was there for some time. It showed signs of salt damage from driving in the winter." So, the doodling was how he organized his thoughts? "I removed them both and bagged them as evidence."

The blonde ADA on the other side of Mollie leaned forward. "If the crime lab doesn't come back with Garner's prints on one of them, we can't prove he put them there."

Mollie realized that Joel had drawn a map of every location where she'd had an encounter of some kind with the man they now suspected was Rocky Garner. He could be placed at the diner, the alley behind it, the dog park, her apartment and Hwy. 40, where he'd met his death trying to kill them. Joel pointed to the symbols where he'd written *RG*. "Then how else do you explain him lying in wait for us when we left K-9 Ranch? We were fifteen miles out of the city, and I know he didn't follow us there."

Kenna leaned back in her seat, shaking her head. She glanced around the table to include everyone in her question. "What else do you have?"

A.J. looked up from his computer. "Garner recently bought himself a thirty-thousand-dollar fishing boat. Paid for in three installments of ten thousand dollars each. The last one was paid yesterday." He turned the screen around to show an invoice from the sporting goods store where Garner had bought the boat. "He's bleeding money in alimony payments to his two ex-wives. No wonder he was keeping the payments out of any bank account. Their attorneys could go after him for more."

"Can we trace the cash?" Kenna was persistent in documenting each fact.

"Not yet. It's already changed hands a number of times. The dealer deposited the payments in his account, and it left the bank shortly after that." A.J. turned the computer back to him and pulled up a different screen. "We can trace the car rental agreement back to Kyra Schmidt. She charged almost six hundred dollars on a credit card to have the car for a week."

Mollie's fingers flinched around the leash. "He's been following me that long?"

"Possibly longer." A.J. looked apologetic when he met her gaze across the table. "There's evidence of other deposits to Garner's account—five hundred dollars, a thousand—some more, some less—over the past two years. It's not overtime pay, because that's direct deposited like his paycheck. It's not from moonlighting as security for a reputable company like a store or sporting venue. The deposits came from Garner himself. That means he took cash to the bank."

Joel reached across the arm of her chair and covered her trembling hand with his own. "Any chance there was a deposit nine months ago?" he asked his supervisor. "That's when he was harassing Mollie at the diner."

"Last October?" A.J. scrolled through the numbers, then nodded.

Mitch Taylor pounded the table with his fist and Mollie jerked in her chair. "I had a dirty cop on my force?" He pulled out his cell phone. "I'm calling Internal Affairs to do a deep dive into Garner's financials."

Joe Hendricks seemed equally disappointed by the proof of Garner's misconduct. "They already have a file of harassment complaints leveled against him."

Mitch muttered a curse. "I have over two thousand employees on the payroll here. And it just takes one bad seed like Garner to give us all a bad rep."

Mollie could appreciate how Garner's actions were an embarrassment to the department, but she had a bigger threat to worry about. "But nothing about Officer Garner ties back to Augie? August Di Salvo?"

It was Joel who answered. "Not yet."

She felt the eyes of everyone in the room looking at her, possibly with pity, but mostly with expectation. It was more than clear that without her help, the Di Salvos would remain untouchable. She tightened her grip on Joel's hand and stroked the top of Magnus's head. "They're setting Kyra up to take the fall if things go south. It's a classic Di Salvo move. With Garner's death, if he was the man they paid to follow me, I think we can safely say things have gone south."

"We'll need a court order to look at Kyra Schmidt's financials." The ADA nodded in agreement with Mollie's assessment. "I'll work on that today. If she's paid Garner to do odd jobs for her and the Di Salvos from her personal account, we can track the timelines to see if they match Garner's deposits. But she could just as easily have paid him petty cash from her law firm, and investigating the firm's financials would be a harder sell to a judge."

Josh Taylor had made a list of crimes on the board. "So, we can prove Garner is guilty of harassment, breaking and entering, and the attempted murder of a police officer and potential witness. We can prove he had some kind of working relationship with Schmidt—"

"Who could get her connection to him tossed out of court by claiming he stole the rental car. Or that she had no idea what he was going to do with it when she hired him for a different job, like escorting an important client to the airport," Kenna countered. "He can't defend himself, thanks to your detective here."

Mollie spun her chair toward the attorney. "Joel saved our lives. If Officer Garner hadn't been driving so recklessly—"

"Easy, Mollie," Kenna apologized. "I'm just repeating what Kyra Schmidt would probably say in the courtroom."

"Don't insult Joel when I'm around. Please. He's a good man. And a good detective. He does whatever is necessary to protect the people he cares about."

"It's okay, Moll." Joel squeezed her hand. "We're just talking through what we know on the case, looking at what all our options are." Then he leaned in more closely and whispered against her ear. "But thank you for sticking up for me."

If they'd been alone, she imagined he would have added something about Cici choosing her drugs instead of protecting him. But they were hardly alone.

"I didn't mean to upset you, Mollie," Kenna apologized, and her blue eyes looked sincere. "I could use someone like you on the witness stand. You speak from a place of strength. You don't come off as someone who's angry or frightened and desperate. You have a calm demeanor."

"Calm?" When was the last time anyone had used that adjective to describe her? "That's because of Magnus."

"It's not just because of the dog. But you could have him in the courtroom with you. You were clearly the wronged party in your marriage, yet you don't sound bitter or brokenhearted."

"I'm more embarrassed that I fell for him in the first place. Trust me, he was easy to get over."

Joel chuckled behind her. Kenna smiled and rolled her chair closer. "I think I like you." For the first time, Mollie felt as if the attorney was speaking to her woman-to-woman, and not as the secret weapon who could make or break her case. "I'd like to take a look at your divorce papers."

"The ones I printed off the internet?"

Kenna nodded. "Sounds like you negotiated yourself a hard deal. And you said it was vetted by an accredited attorney and filed properly, which was a smart move on your part. But maybe I can do better by you."

"I don't want anything from Augie."

"She'd like to be able to teach again," Joel interjected. "Can you get the false report on her record cleared with the school board?"

"I'll waitress for the rest of my life if I have to. I just want my freedom."

"Do you feel free of him?" Kenna asked. "Or are you going to be looking over your shoulder for the rest of your life?"

"Kenna…" Joel warned.

"I'm sorry, Detective. But if I'm going to prosecute this case, and win, I need more than what any of you have shown me." She turned to include everyone in the room. "Garner, I could have put away with my eyes closed. But the DA doesn't prosecute dead men. Maybe I could get Kyra Schmidt fined, or even disbarred, if I could tie her to Garner's harassment campaign. But I've got nothing—nothing—that conclusively links any of this to the Di Salvo family."

"Except me." Mollie felt a little like a soldier being prepped for a suicide mission.

"Look," Kenna began, "I've been in a situation where I wasn't safe. That's how I met my husband, in fact. He saved my life. Twice. That whole situation convinced me to leave the dark side of defense and go to work for the prosecution." She laid her hand on the table close to Mollie, understanding and respecting that she wasn't comfortable being touched by someone she didn't know well. "My point is, I understand your reluctance to put yourself in a position where you feel threatened again. Let me play devil's advocate for a moment. Do you think you're the only person the Di Salvos have threatened? Cheated? Or worse? What about those people who will continue to be hurt by them if nothing is done to stop them?"

"I feel for them, but… Augie said he'd kill me if I left him. I countered with the offer to keep what I took from him out of police hands, so long as he let me leave. And live. If anything happens to me, I've willed it to go to KCPD and the DA's office."

"You're not going to die before we take that bastard down," Joel griped.

But Kenna Parker-Watson seemed eternally cool and unruffled. "It doesn't sound as if he's keeping up his end of the divorce agreement."

Suicide mission. "*If* you can prove he's behind the harassment and Garner trying to kill Joel and me." Mollie offered another explanation. "Kyra Schmidt might have decided to eliminate me to protect her new fiancé and all the money she stands to gain by marrying Augie."

"Possibly," Kenna conceded. "But that just means she knows there's something there she has to protect. You know, the thing about bullies is that they only keep their power when no one stands up to them."

Mollie had heard that argument before. She believed it herself once. "Yes, but the person who stands up to the bully usually gets the crap beat out of them, or worse."

Kenna's hand inched closer. "I'm willing to stand up with you against your bully. You wouldn't be alone this time."

Mollie looked to Joel. He tucked a stray strand of hair behind her ear. "You know I'm with you all the way."

There was a chorus of support from around the room, from A.J. and Josh, as well as the two senior officers. Finally, Magnus put his head in her lap and turned his dark eyes up to hers, promising his unflinching support.

Mollie smiled down into those faithful eyes. Then she lifted her gaze to Joel's handsome golden eyes. She wasn't alone against the Di Salvos. Not anymore. *Not a suicide mission.* Instead, she was the veteran survivor who could lead this makeshift army into battle. She just prayed she wouldn't be a casualty along the way.

She turned to Kenna's blue eyes and nodded to the yellow legal pad in front of her, warning her to get ready to write. "I have documented evidence of money laundering and racketeering from internal servers on the Di Salvo computers. I can show payoffs to enforcers and bribes to officials that probably coincide with the witnesses who backed out of testifying against Augie in his previous trial."

This part was harder. She turned to Joel but couldn't quite meet his eyes. Her gaze landed on the Armed Forces prayer inked into his arm and she replayed the words in her head. *Teach us not to mourn those who have died in the service of the Corps, but rather to gain strength from the fact that such heroes have lived.*

She had to be the hero now. But could she trust that these people would be there for her when she needed them?

Joel tapped a finger beneath her chin and tilted her face to his. "What else, Moll?"

"I don't want you to see them. But I have dated pictures of my injuries and my copy of the first police report and medical exam that disappeared after the first assault. And, there's an audio recording of one of the times Augie…hurt me. There's no video. I hid my phone in a drawer, but it was running the whole time."

She heard deep-pitched curses in two different languages, and gasps of admiration for her and contempt for the Di Salvos from around the room. But her eyes were glued on Joel and the muscle ticking in his jaw at the evidence she'd described. "Hell, babe, you had the presence of mind to record him?"

"That's how desperate I was to get away from him."

His gaze caressed her face. "Strong as steel."

"It's in a lockbox at my bank." She patted Magnus's

shoulder. "I keep the key with me at all times. And the false account numbers are in—"

"Your locket." She nodded at Joel's deduction. "And Magnus guards your key." His eyes remained shrouded in sadness, but he smiled. "Brilliant, brave, and beautiful."

There was a respectful moment of silence before Kenna spoke. "Please tell me you'll let me see that evidence."

She hadn't looked away from Joel. "You'll keep me safe?"

He pulled her into his arms and hugged her as tightly as the chairs allowed. "Twenty-four seven."

"He'll have the backup of the entire Precinct," Joe Hendricks promised.

"Of the entire department if needed," Chief Taylor added. "I'll assign a SWAT team to you to and from the courtroom."

"Are you afraid to testify against your ex?" Kenna asked.

"Yes. But I'll do it anyway. I want…" She reached over to squeeze Joel's hand. "I want to fight for *us*, too."

Chapter Eleven

Joel's head throbbed with a mixture of fatigue and forcing his eyes to concentrate on the pages of the book he wasn't really reading.

For the umpteenth time that night, he let his gaze slide over to the opposite corner of the couch, where Mollie was curled up with her book. He could tell she was deep in thought because she hadn't turned a page in the last ten minutes.

Giving up the pretense, he set his book aside and clicked on his phone to check the time—11:00 p.m. He also pulled up his messages to see if there was any news on what progress the DA's office was making in going through the flash drive, photos, and recording Mollie had turned over when they'd opened her lockbox at the bank the afternoon after that strategy meeting at Precinct headquarters. Nothing there.

He typed a quick text to the undercover officer stationed somewhere outside the house to make sure the neighborhood was as quiet as it seemed to be. Nothing to report there, either.

"Any news?" Mollie finally closed her book and set it on the ottoman in front of them. He hated that there was no hope in her eyes when she looked at him, just polite curiosity.

"No." He tucked his phone into the pocket of his shorts and stood. "It's getting late, though. Maybe we should turn in."

She nodded. "I do have an early day tomorrow."

Mollie had barely slept the past three nights, even with Joel's arms wrapped around her and Magnus snoring on the rug on her side of the bed. There'd been an officer somewhere near them around the clock, and a squad car made regular passes through the neighborhood throughout the night. When they left the house, they both put on protective vests, but here, he thought they were safe enough that they could stay indoors without the vests. Still, he checked the locks on the doors and windows to make sure everything was secure while Mollie roused Magnus and headed back to his bedroom.

He wished there was something more he could do for her to ease the seemingly endless wait for justice to happen.

All she did was work at Pearl's, lie in bed with him, where he'd distract her with kisses and some making out until she fell into an exhausted, if troubled, slumber, and run Magnus through his training paces in the backyard while Kenna Parker-Watson pored over each piece of evidence. Every time she called with a follow-up question, the ADA assured Mollie they were putting together arrest warrants and restraining orders that should put the Di Salvos away for a very long time and give her back the normal life that her marriage had denied her.

Earlier this evening, Joel had declared she needed a break, and he had driven her to Saint Luke's Hospital to visit Corie Taylor and meet her new baby boy, Henry Sid Taylor. Somehow, Chief Taylor and his wife were there visiting, too. But Joel knew the timing was about more than visiting their new grandnephew. Mitch Taylor was armed when he told Joel he'd stand watch outside the room while they visited with Corie, her husband Matt, older son Evan, and baby Henry.

It was a treat to watch Mollie hold Henry, who was a strapping eight pounds and twenty-two inches long, and chat about some of the adventures Corie was missing at the diner. Herb was grumpier than usual with the change in his routine, now that Mollie had stepped in to take over pie baking duty and help with morning prep work. Melissa was looking to hire two new waitresses, with Corie going on maternity leave and Mollie finding a home she was better suited to back in the kitchen. The tourists weren't tipping as well as the regulars, and—thanks to some scheduling by Captain Hendricks—there seemed to be three or four more police officers than usual coming in for lunch or dinner this past week.

Joel loved seeing Mollie smile and laugh with her friend. And watching her hold baby Henry twisted his heart with longing. Mollie would make a great mother with her intelligence, strength, and gentle ways—and he desperately wanted to be the man who put a baby in her belly. If she could ever trust him enough to let him love her.

He'd kept his promise and gone to see Dr. Kilpatrick-Harrison to talk about his nightmares and fears that he wasn't the man that Mollie needed to get through this investigation and trial. Mollie seemed genuinely pleased and relieved that he was taking care of himself.

But it killed him to see the shadows beneath her beautiful blue eyes. Mollie wasn't thinking about babies and a future with him. Until this nightmare was settled, and the Di Salvos were no longer a threat to her, her world was a tiny, confining thing filled with fear and anxiety about living long enough to testify against her ex.

After letting Magnus out for one last run and securing the back door, Joel followed Mollie back to his bedroom. By the time he finished brushing his teeth and pulling off his T-shirt, Mollie was sitting up on the edge of the bed. He walked past her to plug his cell phone into his charger on the bedside table and secure his Glock and holster with his badge in the drawer there.

"You want to get up at 4:00 a.m. again?" he asked, setting the alarm.

She nodded. "I'm still not used to getting to the diner so early. I don't trust myself to wake up on my own."

He smiled down at her. "Then we'd better get to bed now."

She scooted back to the middle of the bed. "You don't have to stay with me. Herb will open the kitchen, and you can drop me off and go on to work or come back home for a nap while I help with prep."

"Twenty-four seven, remember? Where you go, I go." Joel settled in beside her and pulled her into his arms. He loved that she didn't even hesitate to curl against his side and rest her cheek against his chest. When she started tracing lazy circles across his chest with her fingers, he had to capture her hand and spread it flat against his heart to stop his body from reacting to her innocent caresses.

He lay in silence for several minutes, waiting for the tension to leave her body and for her to finally drift off to sleep. But she wasn't relaxing. And neither one of them were sleeping.

"Make love to me, Joel," she murmured against his chest.

"Looking to relieve some stress?" he teased.

But she didn't laugh. "I feel so disconnected from the life I wanted for myself. A career, a man who loves me, a family, a home. I'm this brittle, wishful shell of everything I used to be. But I feel connected to you. I feel closer to who I'm meant to be when I'm with you."

"And you think making love will strengthen that connection?"

"I wouldn't be using you to escape what I'm feeling." She pushed herself up to rest her chin where their hands were clasped and look him in the eye. "I want to be with you because you make me feel stronger."

"Are you sure?" He released her hand to tuck a coffee-colored tendril behind her ear. "Sex could be a trigger for you, and I don't want to make you afraid of me."

"I'd never be afraid of you," she vowed. "And, something might trigger a horrible memory. But I've never wanted to try with anyone else. I've never wanted any man the way I want to be with you."

"I feel the same way. I would be honored—and ever so grateful—to make love to you."

"I can't guarantee I'll be any good."

He pressed a finger to her lips to silence that nonsense. "We're both a work in progress, remember? I might not be any good, either."

She rolled her eyes. "I doubt that. All you have to do is kiss me, and I want you."

"I get the same feeling when you put your hands on me." He raised his head to kiss her gently. She joined the kiss as he rolled her onto her back and he positioned himself beside her. "I expect there to be a lot of talking while we do this. You tell me what you like, and you, for sure, tell me anything you don't like."

"I will." She swept her hands along his biceps and across his shoulders before cradling his jaw between her hands and rubbing her palms against his stubble. "But you need to tell me stuff, too. I want it to be good for you."

"It will be." When she started to protest that he couldn't know that, he silenced her with another, deeper kiss that required several minutes of heated contact before he could pull back and explain. "Because it's with you. Because you trusting me with this is the biggest turn-on and best gift I've ever been given."

She stroked her fingers across his jaw and his heart raced with desire. Her brows arched with an apology. "Protection? I stayed on the pill while I was with Augie because I couldn't imagine bearing his child. But I went off them when I ran out. I've never been with another man, so there was no need to pay for them."

He smoothed his thumb across each eyebrow until she relaxed. She had nothing to apologize for. He'd be honored to take care of her protection in this way, too. "I have condoms."

"Thank you." Her lips were slightly swollen and a seductive shade of pink from their kisses. "I want this so badly. But it scares me, too."

"If you decide you don't want to go through with it, I'll be fine. I'll cuddle with you all night the way we have been."

Her gaze ran down his chest to his belly before she met his eyes again. "Could I touch you?"

"You *are* touching me, babe."

"I mean…" Her hand followed the path her eyes had taken, skimming over his stomach toward the evidence of his arousal tenting his shorts. *"You."*

"You touch me however you want."

He loved it when she laughed like that. He loved when she bravely pushed the boundaries of her growing self-confidence, too. "You'd give me that kind of power over you?"

He loved her, period. "Yes. Don't you know, babe? You always have that kind of power over me."

"You'd better kiss me now, Joel."

"Happy to oblige."

The next thing he knew, her bold hand was slipping inside his shorts and curling around his manhood.

Joel sucked in a harsh breath and gritted his teeth against the jolt of anticipation thundering through his blood. He rested his forehead against hers while he tried to even out his breathing.

She smiled, showing him the woman she'd been before her ex and violence had ever touched her life. "I think we have on too many clothes."

Joel made love to her mouth with his and pulled up the hem of her shirt, taking his time to learn the shape and feel of her breasts plumping beneath his hands. She squirmed beneath his touch, then gasped and arched against him when he plucked her rock-hard nipples between his thumb and palm.

When he lowered his head to lick the exposed peak and draw it into his mouth, her fingers stroked along his shaft. Joel's mind blanked for a moment at the absolute perfection of Mollie's hand on him. "You're going to be trouble for me, aren't you?"

He reclaimed her mouth and gave himself over to her needy hands.

Yeah. So much trouble.

THE MOMENT MOLLIE stuck her key into the back door to the kitchen at 4:50 a.m. the next morning, she knew something was horribly wrong.

It wasn't locked.

She looked up to the man beside her, fearing the worst. "Joel?"

He pressed a finger to his lips, warning her to be silent, even as he unholstered his gun. He pulled his phone from his belt and pressed it into her hands. "A.J. Backup. Now."

Mollie nodded her understanding. She was as afraid now as she'd been that first night Augie had assaulted her. Only this time, her fear was for Joel and the unknown threat that might be waiting on the other side of that door. He gave Magnus a silent hand signal to stay by her side, then wrapped his fingers around the door handle.

She grabbed his arm before he could open it. "Be careful. I don't want to lose you."

He mouthed two words. *"Love you."*

Then he nodded to the phone, pulled open the door, and disappeared inside.

She gaped at the steel door for a moment, processing those last words. Then she snapped herself out of her stunned freeze, galvanized by the emotion filling her heart and spilling over into every cell of her body. Joel loved her.

She loved him.

The rightness of that revelation chased away the self-doubts and second-guessing that had ruled her life for too long. She was fighting for her future, fighting for the man who loved her. She pulled up A.J.'s number.

He answered on the first ring. "Rodriguez."

She didn't bother with a greeting, either. "Pearl's Diner.

Something's wrong. Joel armed himself and went inside to check it out."

"Are you safe?"

"Joel is in there by himself." She articulated every desperate word.

"Easy, Mollie. Backup is en route." He said something to someone on his end, and she pulled the phone away from her ear at the shrill of a siren. "Josh is notifying the UC man assigned to you this morning. We're spread a little thin. Josh and I and a SWAT team are at the Di Salvo estate to take your ex into custody. We've got Mom and Dad in a squad car, but there's no sign of August, Beau Regalio, or the lawyer."

Mollie's heart sank when she heard the jumble of overlapping voices from inside the diner. "That's because they're here."

She jumped back from the door when she heard Joel shouting. "KCPD! Drop your weapon! Hands where I can see them!"

She heard three distinct gunshots. Magnus leaped to his feet and barked. She heard a crashing sound, some indistinct voices…and her name, shouted in a voice that was sickeningly familiar. "Mollie! Where is she?"

She wrapped Magnus's leash around her fist.

"Mollie?" She heard A.J.'s voice over the phone again.

"He needs help. Now!" she shouted.

She disconnected the call and pulled open the door. "Magnus, heel!"

The drops of blood on the floor leading from the back door to the freezer didn't frighten her as much as seeing Beau Regalio dragging Joel's limp body. Was that blood on his shirt beneath the edge of his flak vest? Was this his blood on the floor? Where was Herb?

"Joel!" She would have moved to help, but the gun pressed against her scalp froze her in place.

"There's the little woman." Augie stood at the stainless-steel sinks, wiping his hands on a dish towel. "You've caused me a lot of trouble."

There was no teasing, no love, no regret in his dark eyes as he crossed the kitchen toward her.

The feeling was mutual.

Magnus growled and lunged to her left, nearly pulling her arm from its socket as she fought to keep him at her side. The gun was jerked away from her head as Kyra Schmidt dodged the Belgian Malinois in full protector mode. "I hate dogs!" The blonde backed up several steps until her back hit the row of ovens. "August. We need to take care of business and get out of here now. We need to get to the airport."

"Shut up and keep your gun on her."

Kyra circled around until she was standing in front of Mollie, well out of the furious barking dog's reach.

It was enough of an interchange for her to see Beau dumping Joel inside the freezer and shutting the insulated door. "Joel! What did you do him?" she demanded.

That was definitely blood on the sleeve of Beau's jacket as he pulled up the back of his suit jacket and tucked a Glock 9 mm—probably Joel's gun—into the back waistband of his slacks.

"Did he shoot you?" she taunted. "Maybe Herb went after you with one of his kitchen knives."

"You don't get to talk unless I ask you a question."

She saw it coming, but there was no way to dodge the

fist that came flying at her face. Mollie stumbled back from the blow, and would have landed on her bottom if Magnus hadn't been tugging so hard in the opposite direction. She immediately put her hand up to cup the pain blooming across her cheek. "The police are on their way, Augie. You can't escape."

"I said no talking." He might have hit her once, but Magnus wasn't going to let him hit her again.

Augie cursed. "Get that dog away from me!"

"Shut up, mutt!" Beau kicked Magnus, knocking him off his paws. But he was instantly up and lunging for the bigger man this time.

"Don't you hurt my dog!"

"Put him in the cooler with the others," he ordered Beau. But when the Di Salvo bodyguard tried to grab Magnus's leash, the dog bared his teeth and snapped at him.

When Beau pulled his gun to shoot the dog, Mollie put up her hand, pleading for mercy. "I'll put him in the freezer."

Augie grabbed Kyra's gun and pointed it at Magnus. "Try anything funny and I'll shoot him myself."

Although Magnus fought her every step of the way, she led him through the kitchen. Beau was close enough that she could feel the heat of his big body when he reached around her to open the freezer. When she glanced inside, she saw Herb Valentino lying on the floor, unconscious. There was blood oozing from the bandanna tied around the top of his head. Her heart lurched when she saw Joel lying face down on the floor beside him. A small pool of blood stained the floor beneath him. He was still wearing his protective vest, but one of those gunshots could have hit him in the neck or caught him low in his belly beneath the bottom edge.

Please God, don't be dead. I love you, too.

He'd been shot and left to die once before. Even if she didn't make it out of this, she prayed that backup would come, and Joel would get whatever medical help he needed.

"Quit mooning over your dead boyfriend. Get rid of the dog now!"

Augie's command spurred her into action. "I'm sorry, baby," she apologized to Magnus, forcing him to go against months of training that told him to stay by her side, to be there for her whenever she needed him. "You stay here with Daddy."

He was still barking and lunging for the armed men when Beau shut the freezer. Then he was on his hind legs, frantically scratching at the door to get back out.

Augie grabbed her by the hair. But since she kept it short now, he lost his grip and she fell to the floor. That only seemed to anger him further. Before she could scramble to her feet, Augie took her arm in a painful grasp and dragged her through the kitchen.

"Nobody's coming to save you, Mollie. You're mine. I told you what would happen if you left me."

"Shoot her," Kyra insisted, hurrying after them, her high heels clicking on the tile floor. "We need to make this clean and fast and get out of here."

"I told you to let me handle this."

"I'm a damn good lawyer, August. But even I can't refute a former Di Salvo testifying against you."

"Shut up!" He swung around and backhanded Kyra. *Welcome to the club, lover girl.* "That cop you paid off couldn't finish the job, but I will. I want her to suffer for the embarrassment she's caused me. I lost investors. Father threatened to disinherit me if I didn't get that evidence back. If I'm convicted, we all go down." He barked an order to Beau. "Bring the car around. We'll finish her off at the dump site. Then make sure the charter jet is waiting for us. I intend to be in Belarus where they can't extradite me before any other cop finds me."

Augie's first mistake was that he didn't kill her outright.

His second mistake was in thinking that Magnus was just a dumb, annoying animal of no consequence.

His last mistake was underestimating how determined Joel was to keep her safe.

The emergency latch inside the freezer suddenly unfastened and the door swung open. In three long strides, Magnus was across the room. He leaped at the man holding on to her, his vicious snarl even making Mollie cringe. He hit Augie in the chest with enough force to knock him to the floor and free Mollie. His long teeth clamped around Augie's wrist as he grabbed the dog to fight him off. The gun went flying, clattering across the kitchen and sliding beneath the sink.

"Shoot him! Shoot—" Augie's command ended in a high-pitched screech as teeth tore through flesh.

Beau trained his gun on the dog, but pulled it back just as quickly. "I don't have a shot!" He swung the weapon around at Mollie. "Call off your damn—"

Beau crashed to the floor with a hard thud as Joel tackled him. "Joel!"

The two men fought for control of the weapon. Beau landed a punch in Joel's side that made him groan. But then Joel was on top. He hit the bigger man once, twice, in the jaw, stunning him long enough to flip him onto his stomach, drive his knee into the middle of his back and handcuff him.

Then he pulled his own gun from the bodyguard's belt and turned to Mollie. "You okay?"

She moved behind him as he aimed his gun at Augie. "I'm fine. You got shot."

"Clipped me in the side. Second shot hit my vest and knocked me down. Hit my head. Magnus licked my face. He was quite insistent that I get my ass back out here to protect you."

Augie cried out again.

"Better call him off."

"Magnus! Come!" When the dog didn't immediately respond, she spoke in a louder, firmer tone. "Mama's okay. Come!"

Augie cradled his bleeding arm and writhed in pain as Magnus trotted back to Mollie's side and sat. She picked up his leash and praised him. "Good boy, Magnus. Good boy."

As Joel trained his gun on Augie and ordered him to roll over and put his hands on top of his head, Kyra made a run for the back door. But she was knocked flat on her ass when the door swung open and five fully armed SWAT officers streamed in. They were followed closely by A.J. and Josh, who quickly moved to cuff both Kyra Schmidt and Augie.

Standing down from superdetective mode, Joel holstered his weapon. He reached for Mollie, but she was retrieving a clean towel from the sink shelf. And instead of returning his hug, she pressed the folded towel against the wound in his side. "You're not dying, understand?"

"I'm okay, Moll." He gently grasped her shoulders.

"No, you're not. This is blood. Your blood."

A.J. pulled a whining Augie to his feet while the SWAT

team secured the kitchen and the rest of the diner and helped Herb out of the freezer.

"I see you got yourself shot again, Standage," A.J. commented dryly.

Joel chuckled. "Any bullet you can walk away from…"

"You two, stop it!" Mollie didn't find their cop-to-cop teasing very funny at the moment.

"Don't worry." A.J. handed Augie off to another officer. "An ambulance is on its way. I doubt the bullet hit anything vital or his color would be off, and he'd be unconscious by now. I'm guessing your ex is in worse shape with the damage your dog did to him."

"Magnus did his job. He was protecting me."

A.J. held his hands up in apology. "You'll get no complaints from me. I'm putting that dog in for a medal." Then his eyes darkened with sincere admiration. "Thank you for saving this guy. I need him on my team."

Mollie nodded. "Thank you for being here to back him up."

"Thanks, A.J." Joel pried her hand away from the towel and kept it in place there himself. "Come on. Let's go out front and have a seat somewhere out of the way while they secure the scene."

When she saw that he was limping again, she slipped her shoulder beneath his arm and helped him through the swinging door. Magnus saw his familiar bed at the end of the counter, and she released him so he could sniff it out and lie down if he wanted. Mollie guided Joel to one of the vinyl stools and climbed up on the one next to him.

When she started fussing with the abrasion at his temple, he caught her fingers in his free hand and kissed them. "I'm fine. You just sit here with me and keep the towel pressed against my wound." He frowned when he saw her face, and brushed her hair away from the bruise he must already be able to see discoloring her swollen cheek. "I want them to look at you, too."

"A souvenir from Augie. I've had worse."

"Not on my watch, you haven't."

Tears stung Mollie's eyes as the fear and adrenaline left her body. "You told me you love me, and then you got shot and I thought you were dead."

Joel gently cupped her cheek and swiped away the tears that spilled over with his thumb. "I've been dead. Didn't like it. I've never been more alive than when I'm with you."

Then he slipped his hand behind her neck and pulled her closer until he could cover her lips with his. Mollie reached up to stroke his stubbled jaw and returned the gentle kiss with all the love and hope blossoming inside her. A few moments later, she pulled away to look him in the eye and speak her truth. "I love you, too. I can't wait to testify and put the Di Salvos and their greed and evil out of my life forever. Because I want to start a new life with you."

He smiled. "You want to be part of my pack, Mollie Crane?"

"You'll be part of *my* pack, Joel Standage."

"I accept those terms."

A cold nose nudged her arm, and a warm, furry head nestled in her lap as Magnus squeezed between the two of them.

They both laughed and reached down to pet the dog who had brought them together. "Fine, you big goof," Mollie conceded. "We'll both be part of *your* pack."

* * * * *

Look for more books in USA TODAY bestselling author Julie Miller's Protectors at K-9 Ranch miniseries coming soon. And if you missed the first book in the series, look for Shadow Survivors, *available now wherever Harlequin Intrigue books are sold!*